L. Haren

Then I'll Be Home Free

Novels by Phyllis Anderson Wood

Then I'll Be Home Free

Meet Me in the Park, Angie

Pass Me a Pine Cone

This Time Count Me In

Get a Little Lost, Tia
Win Me and You Lose

I Think This Is Where We Came In

A Five-color Buick and a Blue-eyed Cat

Song of the Shaggy Canary

I've Missed a Sunset or Three

Your Bird Is Here, Tom Thompson

The Night Summer Began (original title Andy)

Then I'll Be Home Free

୬ Phyllis Anderson Wood ୧

DODD, MEAD & COMPANY   New York

1 2 3 4 5 6 7 8 9 10

Library of Congress Cataloging-in-Publication Data

Wood, Phyllis Anderson.
Then I'll be home free.

Summary: The death of Rosemary's beloved grandmother
brings turmoil during her junior year as she and her
grandfather struggle to deal with their painful loss and
Rosemary realizes she must reach out for new relationships.
[1. Death—Fiction.   2. Grandfathers—Fiction]
I. Title.
PZ7.W854Tg   1986   [Fic]   85-27391
ISBN 0-396-08766-3

For Joyce Earnhardt, with thanks

❧ Chapter 1 ❧

Rosemary Magnuson ended the first day of her junior year with a silent wave to her seventh period teacher. She edged her way into the stream of hallway traffic and was swept along by the noisy crowd of students drifting toward the front door. Stepping from the dimly lighted corridors of Glenn High School into the brilliant September sunshine, she felt a little like a mole emerging from its tunnel.

Rosemary shaded her eyes from the glare and surveyed the courtyard scene. Old friends were greeting one another excitedly, eager to exchange news bulletins about their summer vacations or their Labor Day weekends. New freshmen were clustered together, nervously eyeing the opening day rituals.

Remembering the pain of her own first day at Glenn High, Rosemary considered going over to welcome one particularly uneasy group of newcomers. Settling, instead, for an exchange of shy smiles as she passed them, she moved slowly toward the street, feeling guilty and disappointed in herself. She stopped abruptly at the west exit when she heard the voice of Kevin Melero calling to her across the courtyard.

"Hey, Rosie!"

Rosemary winced in embarrassment. How many times had she told Kevin not to call her Rosie? Why did he broadcast that nickname? She blushed, feeling as if a flashing neon sign were pointing her out to everyone in the courtyard. At the same time, though, she had to admit she was amused by the way Kevin could cheerfully work his way around her little rules and regulations.

Rosemary glanced over her shoulder self-consciously and stepped aside to wait for Kevin. He was smiling as he waded through the chattering crowd, greeting people he hadn't seen all summer. When he finally reached Rosemary, he shoved a wayward strand of dark hair away from his face and moved his pile of books to the other arm.

"You walking home?" he asked. "I'll walk with you."

"Not if you're going to call me Rosie!"

Kevin issued a routine "Sorry," as he always did when Rosemary's feelings were bruised. Confidently he fell into step beside her, just as he had been doing for years. Close neighbors since early childhood, Rosemary and Kevin had covered many miles together, creating a comfortable friendship.

"How's it going?" Kevin asked. "Did Cynthia's family get moved to Houston all right?"

Rosemary nodded. "I got a letter from her on Saturday."

"So now you're a shiny new junior without a girlfriend at

Glenn High, huh? I warned you, remember?" Kevin was assuming his big brother manner. "You should've made more friends. Having just one friend is like driving a car without a spare tire." He tossed Rosemary a teasing look. "Just one besides me, that is."

Rosemary was serious. "Kevin, you know how hard it is for me to get acquainted with people."

"That's what you say, Rosemary, but we've been friends for eleven years, and it hasn't been so hard." Kevin glanced at her to see if she was impressed. "Think about it. You were just going into kindergarten and I was starting first grade when my folks moved here." Kevin paused to savor that personal slice of history. "I bet you don't even remember my walking you to school when you were in kindergarten."

Rosemary smiled, recalling the little boy who started each day with his dark hair slicked back with water and a little old-fashioned wave set. His hair was always hanging in his eyes before he reached school.

"We've come a long way together, Rosie . . . Sorry—Rosemary." Kevin was lost for a moment in memories.

"Hey, remember when Tommy Guerrero smeared paste on your face and I came along and beat him up?"

Rosemary chuckled. "If you call getting your nose bloodied and your eye blackened\ beating him up."

"And remember that fourth-grade field trip to the Aquarium, when your teacher took me along because she thought I was good with the younger kids? Your grandma went on that trip, too, as room mother." Kevin's eyes were dancing.

"Uh huh, wonderful with the younger kids!" Rosemary

chuckled. "We all loved it when you dropped your sandwiches into the alligator grotto accidentally on purpose."

"Yeah, and your grandma went to the Aquarium cafeteria and bought me another sandwich." Kevin's tone was almost reverent. "She's some lady! My mother used to say that your grandma had more energy and enthusiasm than any of the other kids' mothers. Your grandpa's great, too," he added.

"I know," Rosemary agreed. "They're pretty lively. It's hard to believe they're almost seventy."

"People are amazed at the way they started all over again, raising you after your parents were . . ." Kevin stopped abruptly, embarrassed that he had wandered off course in his thinking and stumbled into a painful subject.

"It's okay, Kevin," Rosemary said softly, "I can say the words. Killed . . . they were killed, by a drunk driver." She looked at Kevin. "I never knew my mother and father, so I don't really miss them. Grandpa and Gram are my family. Don't worry about it."

"With people like them, who's worrying!"

Kevin's appreciation was obvious. He and Rosemary's grandparents had shared a mutual admiration for years. In fact, Grandpa had a little saying about Kevin: "True blue, through and through, that's what that boy is."

They think Kevin's perfect, Rosemary mused, and Kevin thinks they're terrific. She smiled as she remembered some of the veiled hints her grandparents had dropped recently. They couldn't understand why Kevin was still just a friend, not a boyfriend. She was amused by the thought. Fall in love with the

kid who saw you humiliated with paste smeared on your face?
... who grinned at your knees, raw from tumbling off your first
roller skates? ... who saw you fall off your first bike? ... who
laughed when Calvin Tweedy took you on your first date to a
movie?

Rosemary glanced with a half smile at the comfortable friend
walking quietly beside her, accommodating his long stride to
hers, unaware that she was thinking about him.

Finally Kevin broke the silence. "I want to ask you something, Rosemary." He held his hands up defensively. "Wait,
don't say no. Just say you'll think about it."

"Kevin, I can tell from the opening that it's something I
don't want to do."

"You just don't know you want to, that's all." Kevin gave
her a quick, reassuring smile. "The Newcomers Service Club
needs you," he told her. "You have a way with people."

Rosemary shook her head slowly, but Kevin kept talking.

"New kids are enrolling in Glenn High all the time, a steady
stream of them, from other cities, other states, some from other
countries, not knowing the language or the customs. Rosemary,
all these kids need someone to show them around and be friends
with them."

"I could never do that," Rosemary protested. She could feel
Kevin's smile disarming her.

"I think you'd be good at it," he urged. "You've been a good
friend to me."

"It's just that I've known you a long time. I'm not good at
all with strangers."

"Hey, if you think you're shy, Rosemary, you should see some of our new kids who can't speak six words of English."

Rosemary was beginning to feel terrible. Saying no to any request for kindness was difficult for her, and refusing her longtime friend was doubly hard.

"I'll help in some other way," she apologized. "The Newcomers Service Club is your way. You've had three years with them, learning how to do it, so you can handle everything easily, but it's not something I could do well." She tried to make her voice sound firm and sure. "It's not, Kev."

"Just think about it overnight," Kevin told her in his most persuasive tone. "I know what you're like, and I wouldn't ask you if I thought it would be wrong for you. Okay?" He closed the subject before he got a flat refusal.

By then, they had turned onto Muirwood Way, a quiet street lined with modest tract homes and ornamental plum trees. At the first house on the block, Kevin picked up a newspaper and started up the front walk. He turned back to Rosemary.

"Tell your grandparents hello for me. And if I don't see you in the morning, you can give me your answer after school. I'll meet you in the courtyard."

He waved and went into his house. Rosemary continued to the end of the block, stopping in front of number 300 to admire the brand-new paint job that had cost her grandfather and her so many sore muscles during the summer. She touched some bronze chrysanthemums by the front steps. "Looking good," she told the flowers as she passed.

Rosemary didn't even wonder if her grandparents would be

home. They were always home when school was out. Della Magnuson would be in the sewing room, working on the new dress she had just started. Arthur Magnuson would be in his workshop in the garage, doing one of the repair jobs that he labeled "puttering around." For them, retirement days were as busy as any of their work days had ever been.

"I'm home," Rosemary called as she opened the door.

"I'm in the sewing room," Della replied. "Fix a snack and come join me. But first tell Grandpa you're home. He's been thinking about you all day. I think he's trying to get used to the idea that his favorite little girl is now a junior in high school."

Rosemary smiled to herself and went to the garage door. "Hi, Grandpa."

Arthur was at his workbench, rewiring a lamp. "Oh, good, you're home. How did things go at school?"

"Not bad."

"Classes okay?"

"Mmn . . . yeah, I guess so."

"That's good."

"Kevin said hi to you."

"I like that boy. He's . . ."

"I know." Rosemary cut Arthur off. "True blue, through and through."

They both laughed.

"See you later, Grandpa. I'm starved."

Rosemary closed the garage door and went to the refrigerator for a plateful of snacks and a glass of milk. Then, walking slowly to keep from spilling on the carpet, she went to find her grandmother.

Della looked up from her sewing with a warm smile. "Here's our new junior. How did the first day go?"

"Not bad."

"How are your classes?"

"I'm not so sure about a couple of them—that English class is going to be tough, and the biology teacher requires a big term paper."

"Well, I'm sure you can handle anything you put your mind to, dear."

"Kevin said to tell you hello."

"That's sweet. Is he in any of your new classes?"

"No, but he walked home with me. He's pushing hard to get me to join the Newcomers Service Club."

"Oh? What does that club do?"

"Make new kids feel at home. That kind of stuff."

"I think you'd be a natural for such a club, Rosemary. Newcomers are part of your heritage, you know. Your grandfather and Aunt Sigrid came to America at a young age, knowing very little English, and I must say I found it a very pleasant challenge, helping Arthur learn our language and customs."

Della and Rosemary exchanged smiles that hinted of shared secrets.

"I know, Gram. You thought he was cute. But this is different—I'm no good with strangers."

"Well, it's true that you've always been shy, but now that your friend Cynthia's moved away, I'm afraid you're going to be lonely. The Newcomers Service Club might be a way to meet some new people you'd like. There surely must be a lot of lonely girls who hated leaving their old friends to go to a new school."

Suddenly Rosemary's attention was drawn to the garden outside the sewing room. "Look at that waiting line for the birdbath!" She watched through the window, fascinated. "Did you see that, Gram? One bird's splashing, one's waiting on the edge, and the rest are lined up in the bushes."

"I know, and the line automatically moves forward as each one finishes bathing. I've been enjoying them all afternoon. They seem to be a migratory flock making a rest stop. Such an orderly little crowd!"

"I think your wild birds are your favorite toys, aren't they, Gram?" Rosemary's tone was soft and affectionate.

"Yes," Della replied, "and I'm pleased that you appreciate them, too."

Rosemary smiled at Della and picked up the empty plate. "I'm going to change and go for a run before dinner—unless you need some help."

"Go and enjoy a run, dear. It will clear your head for your English and biology homework."

"Not on the first night, Gram. Please! I thought I'd cut out my new skirt after dinner."

"Oh, that'll be fun. Go change, now, and be on your way," Della urged, smiling to herself.

Recently, Della and her granddaughter had developed a whimsical routine, reminiscent of childhood games, but now played in an adult way. They kept outdoing each other by changing the positions of the animals in Rosemary's old and beloved bear collection. There was always a good chuckle with each new discovery.

In her bedroom, Rosemary caught the teddy bears at their fresh mischief. She had to laugh out loud. This time the bears were on the bed, testing Rosemary's beauty supplies in front of a hand mirror.

I'm so lucky to be raised by grandparents, Rosemary told herself. They're fun. She knew that dinner would bring the three of them together with easy conversation. Then Della would sit nearby companionably while Rosemary cut out her skirt. And finally, at nine o'clock, they would join Arthur for their favorite Tuesday night TV shows.

It was a well-ordered existence in the Magnuson household —a small world of people who had been drawn close by their losses.

๑ Chapter 2 ๙

Kevin's request for help with
the Newcomers Service Club was weighing heavily on Rosemary's mind when she awoke the next morning. The problem
nagged at her all day without any resolution. When the closing
bell rang at two-fifty, Rosemary plunged into the hallway
traffic, nervously rehearsing her final refusal speech on the way
to the courtyard. Kevin wasn't there yet, and she was thankful
for the extra moments to build up her courage.

Rosemary moved to a spot near the wall and watched the
crowd flow past her. Shyly, she exchanged smiles with the
people she knew. And then the smile froze on her face. Kevin
was moving toward her, accompanied by two girls and a young
man. I knew he wasn't going to take no for an answer, Rosemary thought frantically, and now he's set me up so I can't
get away.

"Rosemary, this is Linda Wu," Kevin said. "You know her, don't you?"

Rosemary had often noticed the stylishly dressed girl in her classes, but she had never actually talked to her. Linda had always seemed so quiet that Rosemary was afraid the two of them couldn't keep a conversation going if she started one.

"Hi, Linda," Rosemary replied, embarrassed that she had never spoken to her before.

"And this is Shirley Lee and her brother, Jackson." Kevin nodded toward the other two young people. "The Lees have just arrived from Burma. This is their first day in an American school." Kevin turned back to Linda with an appreciative smile. "Linda speaks Burmese, so she's been translating for Shirley and Jackson."

As Rosemary tried frantically to remember where Burma was, she smiled at Shirley and shook hands with Jackson. "How are you?" she asked, not knowing what to do about conversation through a translator. The Lees smiled back and looked to Linda for clues.

"I'm really sorry that I can't stay around today," Linda apologized to Kevin, "but I only have twenty minutes to get to my dentist appointment. I've written down the directions for their getting home—in both English and Burmese. Can you show them to the bus stop?"

"Sure, Linda," Kevin agreed. "We'll handle it."

I like that "we," Rosemary thought. Not "I'll handle it," but "we'll handle it."

After making some last minute explanations to Shirley and

Jackson, Linda hurried off. Kevin avoided Rosemary's eyes during an uncomfortable moment when no one seemed to know what to do next. Finally, Kevin reached for the paper Jackson was holding and scanned the English part of the directions. He looked up from the sheet, surprised.

"They have to transfer buses!" he told Rosemary. "The 21 bus to Baldwin and then a 12 bus to Carthage."

Rosemary was horrified. "Are you sure they told Linda they'd be okay if we just showed them where to catch the 21 bus?" Her voice trailed off. "What if they get lost? They can't ask for directions . . ."

For a moment, she weighed the possibilities. "We'd better do a little more than point," she finally told Kevin. "Let's at least see that they catch the 21 going in the right direction." She looked up at the Lees, who were smiling bravely. "Come on, Shirley, Jackson, let's go to the bus stop." She motioned for them to follow, and they did.

Rosemary led the way, her self-consciousness overshadowed by the possible hazards to the Lees. The more she considered the situation, the more she began to feel sick inside. The anxieties she had felt during her first days at Glenn High were still vivid in her mind. Remembering how nervous she had been, she wondered how Shirley and Jackson must feel, half a world away from their homeland, holding a sheet of instructions for finding their new house.

Rosemary slowed her pace and dropped back to speak to Kevin, who was struggling to keep a straight face.

"You know, that transfer point is in a tough area," she

whispered. "Some of those guys who hang around on Baldwin like to give people a bad time, especially if they seem new to this country."

Kevin nodded knowingly. Rosemary strode on ahead again, thinking through the possibilities. Finally she turned back to Kevin.

"I really think we'd better go with them their first time, Kev."

Kevin stared at Rosemary. "For someone who says she's no use to the Newcomers Service Club, you're sure making all the right moves!" He smiled appreciatively at her.

"We'll feel better if we do it," she told him. She turned to Shirley and Jackson and said very slowly, "Kevin and I are going with you. On the bus."

The Lees looked confused, but they smiled. Rosemary tried it again, using gestures. Giving up, she said, "That's okay— we'll just get on the bus with you."

Rosemary reviewed the boarding procedures in her mind. "Jackson," she said, "do you have fifty cents in change?"

Jackson studied Rosemary's face.

"Money—two quarters." She pulled out her own coins to show him. Jackson caught on.

"Yes. Fifty cents," he replied. Jackson knew his money. He nudged Shirley to have her quarters ready, too.

"Okay, now say this," Rosemary told Jackson. "I need a transfer, please." He repeated it slowly. "I need a transfer, please." Rosemary looked expectantly at Jackson, who re-peated the sentence again, with a very good accent. Then she waited for Shirley to practice it, too.

"Good. Here comes the 21 bus now. Remember, 'I need a transfer, please.'" Rosemary gave the Lees a reassuring smile as the bus stopped and opened its doors. Jackson and Shirley exchanged glances and climbed aboard. Rosemary and Kevin, following right behind them, grinned with pride as the Lees each said clearly to the bus driver, "I need a transfer, please."

Shirley and Jackson had been so intent on the boarding procedures that they hadn't noticed Rosemary and Kevin boarding, too. When they discovered that their friends were still with them, they gestured and smiled a message that clearly asked, "Do you take the bus home, too?"

"Only today," Rosemary replied.

Shirley and Jackson didn't miss anything on the trip home, quietly pointing things out to each other and occasionally turning to Rosemary and Kevin to share their amusement at some new discovery. They kept careful track of the passing intersections, comparing street signs closely with their written instructions.

As the bus approached Baldwin, Kevin tapped Shirley on the shoulder. "Baldwin's next."

Shirley and Jackson referred again to their sheet and nodded. They turned to say good-bye to Rosemary and Kevin and again were delighted to see their friends following them off the bus.

The Baldwin transfer point was the end of the line for several buses, so the curbs were always lined with waiting passengers. Three bars and some small businesses added customers to the crowd. While Rosemary was thinking what a bad spot it was for a pair of kids who couldn't speak English and who weren't used to America, Jackson and Shirley stood there, quietly composed, taking in the whole scene.

"Did you live in a big city in Burma?" Rosemary asked.

"Yes, Burma," Shirley replied.

"A city or a village?" Rosemary tried again.

Shirley and Jackson looked puzzled. Then Shirley pulled out her dictionary and Rosemary pointed to the English word "city." Shirley read the Burmese equivalent.

"Did you live in a city in Burma?" Rosemary repeated.

Jackson caught it. "Yes. City. Rangoon. Hong Kong, too."

Then they know how to survive, Rosemary thought. She had barely reassured herself, however, when two young men swaggered toward the bus crowd. Rosemary's mind signaled a red alert. She shot a nervous glance at Kevin. Shirley, spotting the pair, tightened her grip on her purse. Jackson watched them warily.

Kevin and Rosemary closed in on the Lees, cutting off the young men's access to them. The menacing pair jostled Kevin a bit as they passed, making it appear accidental, and disappeared into the bar.

"Welcome to the United States of America," Kevin muttered. Shirley and Jackson seemed to accept the encounter matter-of-factly.

"I guess Rangoon and Hong Kong have their bad guys, too," Kevin whispered to Rosemary.

The number 12 bus pulled up, and this time Rosemary and Kevin did wave good-bye to Shirley and Jackson. "Take this bus to Carthage," Kevin told them as they lined up to board.

"Carthage," Shirley repeated.

"Use your transfers," Rosemary added.

"Transfers," Jackson said, nodding toward the ticket in his hand.

"Thank you," the Lees said as they turned to get on the bus. "Good-bye. Thank you."

"Good luck, kids," Rosemary murmured as the number 12 bus, with Shirley's face at the window, turned the corner.

For a moment Rosemary and Kevin continued to stare after it. Then they turned and their eyes met. Suddenly they were speechless, almost embarrassed.

"How did that happen?" Rosemary asked, the strain showing in her voice. "How did that ever happen? One day I'm telling you I couldn't be of any use to newcomers, and the next day I'm standing on Baldwin Street putting newcomers on a number 12 bus. What kind of magic do you work, Kevin Melero?"

Kevin grinned at Rosemary. "You're good," he told her. "You're very good. And you don't even know it. Come on, here comes our return bus."

Kevin and Rosemary were so absorbed in their own thoughts that they didn't talk much on the way home. They both had to get used to the idea of Rosemary's being involved in Kevin's special project. He had counted on modest cooperation, but hardly the total participation he had just witnessed. Rosemary couldn't get over her own surprise at how easily she had assumed a leadership role with the newcomers and how much fun it had been.

As the bus approached their stop, Kevin smiled at Rosemary. "You're okay, Rosie!" he said with a friendly nudge.

Rosemary gently punched him back. "You've had eleven

years to learn my name and you still haven't got it. It's Rosemary, R-O-S-E-M-A-R-Y." The protest was mild this time, lacking the usual conviction.

They walked the two blocks to Muirwood Way in comfortable silence. As Kevin turned into his walk, he said, "Thanks for helping, Rosemary. I know you were hesitant about getting into it."

Rosemary's answer was a shrug of her shoulders and a smile as she walked off. She was thinking how pleased Della would be that her granddaughter's carefully nurtured conscience was hard at work.

Della heard the door open and called, "I'm in the kitchen, dear. Did you have a good day? You're a bit later than usual—any problems?"

"No, Kevin and I just got busy talking with some new kids." Rosemary was saving the whole story until some special moment.

"Your grandpa is in his workshop doing something he hopes will make you happy. He's hard at work refinishing Aunt Alice's old rocker for your room. When you were little, and we visited her apartment, you always loved sitting in it, rocking your teddy bears while we talked."

Rosemary put a hand across her mouth. "Oh Gram, I don't even like that chair now. What I really want is for him to refinish Aunt Alice's old Swedish music box and give it to me."

Della raised an eyebrow. "That's the way it goes, dear. I have a lot of things in this house that weren't exactly what I wanted, but, since I wanted Arthur, I accepted them graciously."

24

Rosemary disappeared into the garage, closing the door to the kitchen. When she reappeared, she whispered to Della, "I think I've just gotten a new rocking chair for my room. I see what you mean."

Dinnertime brought the three Magnusons together again to share one of Della's fine meals. Arthur and Della were eager to talk about school, so Rosemary dredged up an assortment of trivial incidents to entertain them. She didn't feel ready to share the one significant episode of the day. That was something she still wanted to think about alone.

And so, when dinner was finished, Rosemary excused herself and went to her room to "do homework." Alone at last, she flopped on the bed and carefully reconstructed the whole series of events, starting with Kevin introducing the Lees, and ending with Kevin's words, "You're good, Rosemary. You're very good. And you don't even know it."

I didn't think I could do it, she marveled. I really didn't. But the Lees are nice—they're very nice.

❧ Chapter 3 ❧

Rosemary hoped she would run into Kevin on the way to school the next day, because she really wanted to talk some more about the Lees. After a night of thinking about the episode, she was left with the distinct impression that the job simply was not finished. I need to see Kevin, she kept thinking. She saw him several times from a distance, showing new students around the school, but the entire day passed without her ever getting a chance to talk to him.

As Rosemary got busy with her new classes, other pressures pushed the Lees to the back of her mind. Their problems, however, remained there, nagging at her conscience. She knew that someone should take over and offer the Lees friendship. If the Newcomers Service Club was set up to do that, why wasn't the system working? Perhaps Kevin knew something about the situation that she didn't know.

Finding him became Rosemary's top priority the next day. She stopped at his house on the way to school, but he had left early. She watched for him in the halls at every passing period, but their paths never crossed.

Rosemary's uneasiness was mounting. Lunchtime came, and she hung around Kevin's locker for a while, hoping to catch him before he went to eat. When it was apparent that she had missed him again, she headed for the cafeteria, feeling frustrated and a little guilty.

As she passed the library, Rosemary spotted Jackson and Shirley sitting at a table. She stood in the doorway for a moment until she caught Shirley's eye. Shirley poked Jackson, who looked up and smiled, too. Rosemary motioned for them to come out into the hall.

"How's it going? Everything okay?" she asked.

Jackson gestured for her to wait a minute while he dashed back to the table to get their Burmese dictionaries. Then, holding their dictionaries expectantly, Shirley and Jackson waited for Rosemary to speak.

What do I say now? she wondered. What would a dictionary do with "How's it going? Everything okay?" She thought for a moment and rephrased it.

"How are you?"

"Fine, thanks." Jackson had learned the answer to that question.

"Where's Linda?"

Jackson and Shirley each tried to get the other to answer. Finally Shirley got brave. "Linda . . . eat . . . period four."

Rosemary understood. "Oh, Linda has fourth period lunch, and you have fifth period lunch."

Shirley nodded.

"Then why aren't you eating lunch?" Rosemary asked.

She had spoken too fast for the Lees, so she tried again. "Aren't you hungry?"

When they looked uncertain, Rosemary took Jackson's dictionary and pointed to the English word "hungry." The dictionary gave him the Burmese translation, which he told to Shirley. They looked at each other, obviously embarrassed.

"No," Jackson said, "we are not hungry."

"Did you eat lunch in Burma?" Rosemary asked.

"Yes," Shirley replied, "in Burma we eat lunch. We don't eat lunch . . ." She opened her dictionary and made a frantic search, then looked up triumphantly. "We don't eat lunch *today*."

Rosemary was getting suspicious. "Do you eat American food?"

Jackson answered. "Hamburgers? Hot dogs? French fries?" He thumbed through his dictionary for another word. "Sometimes."

By then, Rosemary knew she wasn't getting the whole story. "Are you afraid to go to the cafeteria?"

Shirley opened her dictionary. "No, not afraid." She flipped the pages again. "But we will look . . . foolish."

"People laugh," Jackson explained.

"No, they won't!" Rosemary, feeling suddenly protective, looked for a quick ally. "We'll find Kevin, and we'll all eat together, and no one will laugh." She hoped it would be as easy as she made it sound.

"The money . . ." Jackson pulled out his wallet. "Do we have the money?" he asked.

"Yes, more than enough. You can eat twice."

Rosemary was surprised at how well the conversation was going. They were understanding each other without difficulty. Suddenly she drew back. How come on Wednesday these kids acted as if they couldn't speak a word of English, and today they're carrying on a conversation? Have I been taken in? Rosemary's eyes narrowed.

"Hey!" she said tartly, "I thought you didn't know any English." She studied Shirley and Jackson suspiciously, wondering if she was making an idiot of herself.

Jackson met Rosemary's eyes with openness and answered deliberately, picking his words with care. "We don't speak English very much in our class. We only translate English books. We aren't good to talk."

"You studied English in Rangoon?"

"No, in Hong Kong. We are . . ." Jackson flipped the pages of his dictionary. "We are . . ." He groped for a word.

"Embarrassed," Rosemary prompted.

"Yes, embarrassed . . . We are embarrassed to speak. We live in Hong Kong only short time. We are not good to speak."

"You will be good," Rosemary said. "Trust me, you will be." She had just seen the possibilities. "Right now you're going to learn all about the great American school cafeteria. Put your books in your lockers, and let's go."

As they opened their lockers, Shirley giggled at some comment Jackson made in Burmese. Then, with their books out of the way, the trio headed for the cafeteria.

"Let's look for Kevin," Rosemary said as they entered the noisy, steamy cafeteria. Shirley quickly spotted him at a far table.

"Wait here," Rosemary said. "I'll get him to save us some seats."

Kevin had seen them enter the cafeteria. Grinning, he watched Rosemary weave her way over to him.

"How'd you manage to get the Lees here?" Kevin sounded impressed. "They told me they didn't eat lunch."

Rosemary shrugged her shoulders smugly. "Save us three seats, will you?"

"Sure."

Rosemary hurried back to Jackson and Shirley and led the way to the food service. The Lees studied everything around them as they stood in the slow-moving line—the people, the food on other people's trays, the procedures.

"Will you . . . teach the foods?" Shirley asked. "In the store . . . I look at pictures . . . I buy wrong foods."

"Sure, Shirley. Some day we can go to the supermarket. Right now, let's start with cafeteria food." Rosemary started to laugh. "If you can stand it," she added.

Jackson's face clouded over with confusion. "Stand?" he asked. "Stand the food? Stand means . . . get up . . . yes? To not sit down?"

"Usually it does," Rosemary explained, "but in this case it means to put up with." Then she realized the second explanation meant no more than the first. "To stand the food means liking it just a little, or not hating it."

Rosemary marveled that newcomers could learn English at all, with its craziness and traps she had never been aware of before.

Systematically, she began pointing out foods and saying their names, while Shirley and Jackson repeated them softly to themselves. By the time they reached Kevin with their trays, the Lees knew an English name for every food on their plates.

"They're learning fast," Rosemary announced to Kevin with a trace of pride in her voice. "We're doing it again on Monday. And someday I'm going to a supermarket with them and give them hundreds of new words—well, dozens, anyway."

"Better buy a notebook . . ." Kevin started to suggest to the Lees. Before he could go on, both of them reached for their dictionaries. Soon they repeated the word notebook with understanding.

"Buy a notebook," Kevin continued, "and each time you learn a new word, write it in English and Burmese. You'll learn words quickly."

Shirley and Jackson were glowing with enthusiasm when the bell rang for sixth period. "Thank you for your help," Jackson said. Shirley nodded agreement.

"I'll meet you near your lockers on Monday at the start of fifth period," Rosemary told them.

"Yes, fifth period," Jackson repeated.

"I'll be there, too," Kevin added. "See you."

"See you," Shirley echoed as she and Jackson headed for their sixth period classes.

"I probably won't see you after school today," Kevin told Rosemary as they left the cafeteria. "I have some errands to do for my mom before I go home. But I'll meet you for lunch on Monday."

It was time to make a last-minute dash to sixth period. Kevin, starting down the hall, turned and shouted back, "You were terrific, Rosie!"

He was well beyond hearing as Rosemary started her protest, "My name is . . . Yeah, right. Thanks, I guess."

Kevin's praise had given her morale a boost. She hoped he would show up after school to walk at least partway home with her. For once she would even have welcomed his "Hey, Rosie." She really wanted to hear him say once again, "You're good, Rosemary—you're very good," for she had begun to tell herself that maybe, just maybe, Kevin was right.

৯ Chapter 4 ৎ

By the time Rosemary arrived home, she was eager to share the whole story of the Lees with her grandmother. She'll love it, she thought. She'll be proud that some of her Gunderson traits are showing up in me.

"I'm home," she called as she opened the front door. When Della didn't reply from the sewing room, Rosemary followed the sound of running water. She paused in the kitchen doorway, not sure why she suddenly felt a chill pass over her.

Arthur was standing at the sink, washing vegetables. Afternoon sunshine filtered through the filmy curtains, turning his hair into a crown of silver. When he turned to greet Rosemary, his wrinkled but handsome face looked drained.

"Where's Gram?" Rosemary asked.

Arthur wiped his hands and motioned for her to sit down at the table with him.

"The doctor is running some tests," he said in a carefully controlled voice. Rosemary noticed his hands trembling as he clasped them together.

"Where is she, Grandpa? What's happened?" Rosemary's panic was growing.

"She's in Mercy Hospital. During the morning she started having chest pains, so I drove her right to the emergency room, where they took care of her. By two o'clock the pain subsided, and she was resting quietly, so she insisted I come home to be with you."

"What's wrong with her?"

"The doctor said it was a slight heart attack and that I had done the right thing by getting her to the hospital immediately." Seeing the panic in Rosemary's eyes, Arthur hurried to re-assure her. "People survive slight heart attacks, you know."

"I want to see her, Grandpa."

"I told her we'd eat and then come to the hospital for a visit after dinner. Della wouldn't hear of me staying there with her and leaving you alone, worrying. You know how your grandma is."

Rosemary nodded. "I know." She went to a drawer and got the garden clippers. "I'll cut some flowers to take to her. How about the Shasta daisies with some asparagus fern?"

"Sounds fine."

"Are you sure she's all right, Grandpa?"

"No, I'm not at all sure."

"Let's not bother with dinner—let's just get there," Rosemary urged.

"No, I promised Della I'd give you a good dinner, so that's what I'm going to do." Arthur returned to the sink. "Why don't you pick the flowers and get some of your homework done while I fix the dinner? It won't be long."

Rosemary chose the finest of the white daisies, added a few pink daisies, and softened the effect with green fern. She smiled with satisfaction as she put the bouquet in water until it was time to leave. Then she went to her room to try to study. Finding it impossible to concentrate, she gave up and returned to the kitchen.

"How did she look this afternoon, Grandpa?

"Pale. Very pale. But she's clearheaded."

"Does she want anything? I'd better get her robe . . . slippers . . . comb." Rosemary went to pack some of her grandmother's belongings.

"Dinner's ready," Arthur called in a few minutes.

"Be right there, Grandpa." Rosemary came into the kitchen, sat down opposite Arthur at the table, and stared in surprise at the meal he had served. "Grandpa, this is a great dinner!"

"When you've cooked in the shadow of Della Gunderson Magnuson, you have to do it right," Arthur replied, a smile brightening his face for a moment.

They began to eat, but neither of them had much appetite. Several times Arthur started to say something, but lost the thread of his thought. Finally, he lapsed into total silence.

Rosemary didn't feel like talking, anyway. She was torn between her anxiety about what she might find at the hospital and her concern for a new kind of stress that she was noticing in her grandfather. The old man had his eyes fastened to his plate.

When they both had eaten as much as they were going to, Rosemary stood up, hoping to bring Arthur's attention back to the meal.

"I'll serve us some ice cream, Grandpa." She took their plates to the sink and opened the freezer door.

"Chocolate chip or raspberry sherbet?" She glanced at her grandfather, waiting for some sign of acknowledgment. Arthur was still remote.

"Right!" Rosemary said with forced enthusiasm. "Raspberry it is." She set a dish of sherbet in front of the old man and watched him automatically pick up a spoon and eat the sherbet, seeming unaware of what he was doing.

Rosemary was becoming unnerved. Her grandfather, who always prided himself on his control, was in some other world, out of touch. She made a cup of instant coffee and set it in front of him, then cleared the table and washed the dishes. The old man sipped his coffee slowly.

When the cup was finally empty, Arthur leaned back in his chair, rubbed his eyes, blinked a few times, and snapped back suddenly to the scene in the kitchen. He looked over at Rosemary, standing at the sink, and expressed concern.

"You're awfully quiet, Rosemary. Are you all right?"

"Sure, Grandpa."

"You're looking a little pale."

"I'm just worried about Gram."

"So am I. Let's get over to the hospital. I'll be ready as soon as I get my keys," Arthur said.

In a moment he was wandering around, searching for his car keys.

"Did you move my keys, Rosemary? They were right here on the TV. I always leave them on the TV."

"No, I haven't seen them."

"Look in your purse. I'll bet you picked them up thinking they were yours."

Rosemary was getting worried about the way her grandfather looked. Beads of sweat had broken out on the old man's forehead, and his face was flushed. It was unlike Arthur to go to pieces over things. Rosemary emptied her purse just to satisfy him.

"We can use my keys for now," she offered. "Yours will show up. Here." Rosemary held out her car keys. "Let's visit Gram."

"I want to find my own keys," Arthur fussed. "I don't like unfinished business."

"We'll finish it," she assured him. "We'll just do it later, not now."

Mopping his brow with a handkerchief, Arthur grudgingly accepted Rosemary's keys and started down the steps. A sharp gust of wind hit him, standing his white hair on end.

"For pete's sake," Rosemary yelled from the doorway, "get a coat!"

That command did it. Arthur exploded. "Do you think I'm a child? I guess I'm capable of deciding when I want a coat. I don't need a teenager telling me how to dress."

Rosemary bristled. Her grandfather never spoke to her that way. "Okay, Grandpa, be stubborn it you want. Catch pneumonia!" She slammed the front door for emphasis. The minute the words were out, Rosemary wished she hadn't said them.

Arthur, by then, was fumbling with the key, unable to get it into the car lock. Rosemary, genuinely sorry for her outburst, groped for a way to make peace.

"Here, Grandpa, I'll drive for you."

"I'm not senile!" Arthur snapped. "I can still drive a car."

Rosemary was stunned by her grandfather's rebuff. It was so out of character. I wish I hadn't said that about catching pneumonia, she thought. What if he really does? Her mind raced ahead in panic. Gram with a heart attack. Grandpa with pneumonia? Oh please, God, no! Rosemary was sick with remorse.

"I just wanted to help," she told her grandfather, her voice weak from the vision of losing the only family she had. "I just wanted to make things a little easier for you tonight, that's all. You go ahead and drive, Grandpa."

Arthur got into the driver's seat and Rosemary slid in beside him. She noticed his hands trembling, but said nothing as he put the key into the ignition, backed out of the driveway, and drove down Muirwood Way. Then he overshot his lane turning onto Maple and had to pull sharply to the right to avoid an oncoming car. Rosemary sucked in her breath and struggled to maintain her silence.

Halfway down the block Arthur pulled over to the curb. "I believe I'll let you drive, Rosemary," he said. "I'm feeling a bit tired."

"Sure, if you want, Grandpa. You slide over, and I'll come

around." She got out of the passenger side and went to the driver's side. Looking anxiously at Arthur, she pulled the door closed, observing how the color had drained from his wrinkled face, leaving his skin ashen.

"You okay?" she asked softly.

Arthur nodded and leaned his head back on the headrest.

"It's getting to you, having Gram in the hospital."

"I'm afraid you're right."

Rosemary didn't push the conversation. She drove in silence, taking extra care not to jolt the old man who rode beside her with his eyes closed and his hands resting limply in his lap.

As Rosemary turned into the Mercy Hospital parking lot, Arthur opened his eyes. He watched with silent admiration as his granddaughter expertly eased the car into a badly angled parking space.

"Rosemary," he finally said, almost in a whisper, "forgive me for sounding like a cranky old man."

"Forget it, Grandpa. I'm sorry I yelled at you about the overcoat, too."

"It's just that I'm so worried about Della," Arthur said softly.

"I know, Grandpa . . . I know." Rosemary put a hand on Arthur's bony knee. "Me, too."

ঌ Chapter 5 ২

As Rosemary and Arthur en-
tered the hospital, the warmth of the lobby engulfed them,
softening the edge of their raw feelings. Once inside the building, they both sensed more clearly what was required of them.
Della was upstairs, and their job was to visit her, reassure her,
bring her cheer. Rosemary tidied up her flowers and smoothed
her windblown hair. Arthur paused by the lobby mirror and
glanced toward the gift shop.

"Do you think I should get her something?" he asked Rosemary. "Some cologne or lotion or anything?"

"Well . . ." Rosemary was unsure, too. "We have the flowers
tonight. That's probably enough."

"I guess so." Arthur seemed satisfied.

They moved on toward the elevators, uneasily anticipating

the scene to come. At the fourth floor, the silent pair followed the juice cart down the hall to the east wing and paused outside room 4211. Arthur entered first, with Rosemary trailing nervously behind.

Della, in the bed by the window, appeared to be sleeping, her eyes closed, her breathing heavy. Rosemary put away the few things she had brought her grandmother, while Arthur pulled up a chair and took Della's hand in his, unconsciously rubbing his thumb back and forth across her wide gold wedding band as he studied the pale face. Della slowly opened her eyes and smiled at Arthur.

"Oh, I'm so glad you came," she said softly. "I was just thinking about you."

Arthur's eyes filled with tears.

"Did you manage to get dinner?" Della asked. "Is Rosemary all right?"

"I'm right here, Gram." Rosemary put a hand on her arm.

Della turned her head toward her granddaughter. "How sweet of you to come with Grandpa. It's a school night, and I know how busy you are. Did you have time to go running?"

"No, but that's okay." Rosemary thrust the daisies toward her. "I thought you'd want some flowers, Gram, but I see you've already gotten a bouquet from the church."

"I like your flowers better, dear. Maybe you can get a vase to put them in."

"Sure, I'll go find something."

As Rosemary left the room, Arthur stood up to kiss Della.

"I keep worrying about you and Rosemary," she murmured.

"Well, we do miss you," Arthur replied. "But you mustn't worry. We're very competent."

Rosemary returned with the daisies in a cardboard milk carton. "I'll bring a vase from home tomorrow," she promised.

"Rosemary, you can take my seat here," Arthur said. "I want to find out about the doctor's report."

They exchanged places, putting Rosemary in a position where her grandmother could see her more easily.

"How are you doing, Gram?" she asked chattily.

Della put on a brave smile. "I'm trying to be a good patient so I can get home soon." Then she turned serious. "Rosemary, you will take care of Grandpa, won't you? He's not young anymore."

"Sure, Gram. I'll take good care of him until you get home." Rosemary patted her grandmother's hand comfortingly.

Della nodded. "I know I can depend on you. So now, tell me how things are going at school."

"Okay, I guess. Kevin will be worried about you when he hears you're in the hospital."

Della was pensive. "I wish you could see how remarkable that young man is, Rosemary. He's always been so good to you, and you've just taken him for granted."

Rosemary shrugged. "He's okay. I have to admit that. But he's always been around."

Della chuckled. "I hope long-lasting friendships aren't out of style these days. Your grandpa and I started out as good friends, and . . ."

The juice cart interrupted the conversation. Della selected a can of apple juice, and Rosemary held it for her while she sipped it with a straw. When she had finished, she motioned for Rosemary to come close.

"Much as I love having you both here," she whispered, "I want you to take your grandfather home now and try to get him to rest. He needs sleep. He looks exhausted."

Rosemary nodded. "I know, Gram. I'll try."

Della pulled her close again. "I know he's a hard one to give orders to."

Rosemary nodded emphatically.

"But you're a Gunderson," Della went on with a sly little wink. "I'm sure you can find ways to protect him against himself."

"Like you always have, you mean?" Rosemary gave her grandmother a playful little punch on the arm.

Arthur walked in at the end of this exchange. He could see that the two of them were involved in one of their little conspiracies against him, but he was glad for anything that could bring some animation to Della's face.

"Grandpa," Rosemary said in an urgent tone, "I just remembered I have to outline a chapter for history. I've got to be getting home."

"Tomorrow is Saturday. You'll have time, won't you?" Arthur looked baffled.

"I forgot this assignment, because the teacher told us about it on Tuesday. And I have so much work for my other classes besides." Rosemary knew her explanation sounded lame.

Arthur didn't argue. "Della, will you excuse us if we have to cut our visit short? Your granddaughter doesn't wish to fail history and be a junior twice."

"Right. Once is plenty."

Arthur patted Della's hand and stooped to kiss her again. "Hurry home, Lady . . ." he murmured. Then, becoming so choked that he couldn't finish, he turned away quickly.

Rosemary and Della exchanged a secret success sign between themselves.

"Good-bye, dears," Della said with a little wave. "Thank you for coming. I loved having you here."

Returning her wave, Arthur and Rosemary left the room and headed down the hall. Neither dared to speak. They rode the elevator in silence and left the building in silence. They drove for three blocks without a word.

At last Arthur looked over at Rosemary, who was moving through the traffic with skill. "Tell me the truth," he said. "Do you really have that much homework?"

"Well . . . the outline is due. And I do have some other homework besides. But it's not that much, really."

"Then why did you use that as an excuse to leave?"

"Because Gram wanted me to think up some way to get you home early. I'm supposed to see that you get some sleep."

"So why are you letting me in on the plot?"

"Because nobody in this world but Della Gunderson Magnuson can make you do something you don't want to do, Grandpa. There's no point in my telling you to get some sleep—you'll do what you want."

"Are you saying I'm a stubborn old mule?"

"Mmn . . . stubborn, maybe."

For the first time since Della's heart attack, Arthur Magnuson laughed. He laughed until tears rolled down his cheeks. And when the tears kept rolling, Rosemary handed her grandfather the tissue box from the glove compartment.

By the time they reached 300 Muirwood Way, Arthur was truly ready to sleep. He went right to bed and soon was snoring heavily. Rosemary, on the other hand, wasn't sure she could sleep at all. Her new realization that her grandparents might not last forever left her numb.

With Arthur asleep, the house seemed cold and empty. Rosemary, feeling a sudden rush of loneliness, gave up on her homework and turned on the TV, but after flipping channels idly, soon gave up on that, too. Sprawled in the armchair, she felt suspended between worlds, disconnected from everything.

Finally, she picked up the phone and called Kevin to tell him the news.

"Kev, Gram's in the hospital . . . Slight heart attack, they said . . . No, Grandpa's already asleep, and I'm going to bed soon, but thanks for offering . . . No, I don't think there's anything for you to do . . . I know you would . . . I guess I just needed to tell a friend . . . Yeah, you are, Kev, a good one . . . I know you would . . . Thanks . . . Bye."

When Rosemary hung up the phone, she felt a little less alone. Kevin would be here in two minutes if I ever needed him, she told herself. With that security, she turned out the last light in the house and went to bed. In the darkness, she took comfort from the sound of Arthur's rhythmic snoring in the bedroom across the hall.

Rosemary tossed and turned in her bed, trying to will herself into sleep, but her worries were too real to be put aside. The whole weekend, she kept thinking. I may need Kevin much sooner than he expects. How will I get through a weekend?

Rosemary opened her eyes the next morning and stared at the soulful face of Benjamin Bear. "It's Saturday," she whispered to him, "and I wish it weren't. Gram says I'm supposed to take care of Grandpa. But for a whole weekend?"

Apprehensively, she dressed and wandered down the hall. She found Arthur in the kitchen, washing his breakfast dishes. When he saw her, he smiled wanly.

"I'm going to leave right away and spend the day with Della," he told Rosemary as he dried his hands. "I'll take a book along and just be there whenever she wants something." He glanced uncertainly at his granddaughter. "Will you be all right?"

"Of course, Grandpa."

"That will be Della's first question. She'll scold me for leaving you in order to stay with her."

"Tell her I'll outline my history chapter this morning. It'll please her that I'm sounding studious. And I'll come to visit her this afternoon."

"But I'll have the car," Arthur worried.

"I'm a big girl, Grandpa. I can take the bus, or, if Kevin can borrow his mother's car, I know he'll drive me down. I'll be fine. Worry about Gram instead of me."

"I am, Rosemary. That's why I want to stay with her."

Arthur's tone left Rosemary feeling nervous. Her brave

words sounded hollow to her as Arthur drove off, leaving her alone in the house. I'll get busy, she thought. I need to keep occupied. She made her bed and then opened her history book. As she stared at the pages, the words became blurry and the sentences disconnected.

It was clear that the history homework was going to have to wait. I'll have to keep busy some other way. I'll call Kevin, she decided. I think I need him. Rosemary dialed his number and waited a long time for an answer. When a voice did respond, Rosemary recognized Kevin's older brother.

"Hi, Stan; it's Rosemary Magnuson. I thought you were in Dallas . . . How's the new business going? . . . That's good . . . Kevin's gone till Sunday night? No, no message. Bye, Stan."

That's that, Rosemary told herself as she hung up. You're on your own until Monday. Good luck, kid. She began wandering through the house, tidying up a few things, throwing out others, until finally she gave up and left for the hospital.

After the long bus ride, the visit was a total disappointment to Rosemary. She didn't even get to talk to her grandmother because Della slept soundly the whole time she was there. Disconsolately, Rosemary returned home and waited out the time until her grandfather would return home for the night. She fixed a simple supper, setting his aside and taking hers into the living room.

Several hours of TV programs passed in a blur before she finally heard Arthur opening the garage. She hurried to meet him at the door, anxious for an updated report.

"Did Gram wake up after I left?"

"Yes, finally. She was touched that you'd gone to the trouble of coming all the way down by bus to see her."

"Is she okay?"

"I can't tell, Rosemary. She seems to be sleeping a lot." Arthur dropped his jacket on the chair.

"Want some tired supper, Grandpa?"

"No, I ate most of Della's dinner because she didn't want it, but thank you, anyway. I'm so exhausted that I'm just going straight to bed. Sorry I'm such poor company." Arthur moved with slow steps through his bedtime routine, and soon Rosemary heard him snoring.

Sensing the lack of reassurance in her grandfather's report, Rosemary embarked upon another troubled night.

When morning came, she quickly discovered that Sunday wasn't going to be any better, for Arthur was leaving early again to spend the day with Della.

Rosemary went to the hospital by bus later in the morning to join the bedside vigil, only to be disappointed because her grandmother didn't wake up to visit with her.

Finally, after a long afternoon of waiting in the lonely house for her grandfather to return, Rosemary decided to eat dinner alone. It was early evening when Arthur did arrive, tired and depressed. Before he could take off his jacket or sit down, his granddaughter started plying him with questions, most of which couldn't be answered satisfactorily.

"How's Gram?"

"I wish I knew, Rosemary. She felt cheated that she missed your visit again—wanted to know why I didn't awaken her."

"Did you tell her you tried?"

"No, that would have distressed her."

"What did the doctor say?"

"Not much, really. That we have to wait and see what kind of progress she makes."

"Is she worrying about us?"

"I'm sure she is, Rosemary."

"But I told her I'd take good care of you, Grandpa."

"And I told her I'd take good care of you, too."

"I wish we could do more for her."

"So do I, Rosemary. So do I."

"Want me to fix you something to eat, Grandpa? Some hot chocolate, maybe?"

"No, thanks. I ate at the hospital. Actually, I just want to go to bed and get some sleep."

Arthur headed for the hallway, then turned back to his granddaughter. "You'll excuse me, won't you, Rosemary? I'm not very good company these days, and I'm sorry."

"That's okay, neither am I. Get some sleep, Grandpa. You need it."

Rosemary turned out the lights in the house and retreated to her room.

Alone, hugging Benjamin Bear, she prayed.

❧ Chapter 6 ❧

Monday morning finally dawned, but after a restless night of tossing and turning, Rosemary almost wished she hadn't gone to bed. She turned off her alarm and stumbled into the bathroom for her shower. Dressed for school, she headed for the kitchen, expecting to find her grandfather fixing his ritual cup of coffee. The kitchen was untouched. With a nervous fear tightening her throat, Rosemary hurried to the bedroom to see if Arthur was all right.

The old man was snoring steadily, his chest heaving with each breath. Rosemary stood in the doorway, letting her throat loosen up. It took a while. Never before in her life had Rosemary ever thought to worry about whether her grandfather was still breathing or not.

A soft knock at the front door brought Rosemary back to the moment. Her whole body tensed up, anticipating a message about Della. No, that's silly, she told herself. Bad news would come by phone, not messenger. Her body went limp. Pulling the bedroom door closed so Arthur wouldn't be disturbed, she went to the front door.

Kevin was standing on the porch holding a towel-wrapped package.

"Have you had breakfast?" he asked.

"Kevin, my brain has barely started to move. I haven't begun to think about my stomach yet." There was a note of irritation in Rosemary's voice.

Kevin was undaunted. "My mom made some cinnamon rolls for your breakfast. We figured you'd both be kind of down this morning after a long weekend with your grandma in the hospital. She's still there, isn't she?"

"Oh, Kevin—" Rosemary searched for words. "Yes, she is." Her conscience was bothering her, as it so often did when she hadn't been very responsive to Kevin. "Come on in. That was nice of your mom—and you." Rosemary peeked under the towel with new interest and carried the container to the kitchen. Kevin followed her.

"Grandpa is still asleep, but I'm going to eat right now," Rosemary said, keeping her voice down. "Want to join me?"

"Naturally!" Kevin was already at the table. "I wouldn't want you to have to eat alone."

Rosemary sat down at the table, then started to jump up. "Want some juice or milk or something?"

"What is this?" Kevin asked, pushing her gently back into the chair. "I can handle that much, I hope." He poured milk and juice for both of them, while Rosemary unwrapped the rolls. The fragrance of the fresh bread filled the kitchen.

"I thought today was going to be a total loss," Rosemary commented, "but these cinnamon rolls just might save the day." They both reached for a roll at once. Rosemary's hand stopped in midair. "We'd better set some rolls aside for Grandpa before we start in on them."

"Yeah, I think we'd better," Kevin agreed, laughing.

Hoping her grandfather would feel like eating heartily, Rosemary wrapped up five rolls and set them on the counter. As an afterthought, she wrote a label and propped it up against the rolls:

FOR GRANDPA—FROM GUESS WHO

In little letters at the bottom, she added, "Your clue: true blue, through and through."

Kevin peered over at the label and grinned. "You mean the cinnamon rolls are true blue?" he teased.

"No, Kevin." Rosemary sounded as if she were teaching something to a first grader. "Try again. Think hard."

Kevin was suddenly shy. "You mean I'm true blue."

Rosemary pointed a finger at him. "Bingo. You got it."

Kevin beamed and turned his eyes away. "That's nice, Rosemary, really nice."

Rosemary sat down again and reached for a roll.

"Tell me about your grandma," Kevin said.

"There's no new report." Rosemary paused, trying to sort out her feelings. "But I suspect she's worse than she's willing to admit, or than Grandpa's willing to admit."

"Maybe you just haven't seen her sick very often, so it's more scary for you," Kevin suggested.

"Maybe," Rosemary agreed. She wanted to believe that.

As the supply of rolls dwindled, Rosemary began to come to life. "Those were great. Tell your mother they were a wonderful surprise." She leaned back contentedly. "I sure needed something to get me started this morning."

"I figured you would. You just realized last night that people don't last forever, didn't you?"

Rosemary looked at Kevin in amazement. "How did you know that?"

"My dad died—remember?"

Rosemary turned away, embarrassed by her clumsy question. Kevin started tidying up the kitchen, and Rosemary silently joined him.

"I'll check to see if Grandpa is awake," she said as she dried her hands. "Then we'd better get going. Mr. Hazeltine acts as if it's a federal offense to be late to his class."

"Yeah, I've heard about him," Kevin said. "I have Mrs. Lozada, and she's always putting work on the board when the bell rings, so it's easy to sneak in."

Arthur was still sleeping soundly, so Rosemary and Kevin tiptoed out and closed the door softly. While they were walking, Rosemary's mind drifted back to other mornings, some of them long past.

"You always have been an early morning person, haven't you?"

Kevin grinned at Rosemary's observation, wondering just what she was recalling.

"I remember, early in the mornings, while I was still yawning, you used to be out on the sidewalk riding your bike." Rosemary was sifting memories. "And later we had our paper routes—yours was a morning one, naturally, and mine was afternoon. And now, you go running before breakfast while I'm simply trying to start my engine for the day."

"That's true," Kevin agreed, "but when you've finally gotten into stride, I'm winding down. I wouldn't try running in the evenings the way you do."

"I guess it evens out somehow," Rosemary decided. "You'll probably end up in a day job, and I'll go for the night shift."

Kevin chuckled. "Something for everyone."

"Anyhow, I'm glad you're a morning person today," Rosemary said emphatically.

They continued to reminisce comfortably until they reached the school. As they paused in the main corridor in front of the office, Kevin brought up the subject of the Lees.

"Are we still meeting Shirley and Jackson at lunchtime the way we planned?"

"Sure."

"Great! That's really great!"

Kevin's response struck Rosemary as too enthusiastic, but before she could figure out why she thought so, he went on.

"I think it's terrific that you've joined the Newcomers Service Club, Rosemary. I knew you were right for it."

Kevin's assumption triggered a surprise attack from Rosemary. With the lack of sleep and the intense worry over Della, her nerves were raw and her emotions near the surface.

"Wait a minute, Kevin!" she steamed. "Where did you get the idea that I'd joined a club? You know it's my way to do things alone. I'm not a group person. I never have been, and I never will be. I thought you understood that." Rosemary's overreaction was rapidly getting out of hand. "Don't go jumping to conclusions. Just because I made friends with two new kids, it doesn't mean I'm joining something. You're good at organized kindness, but I'm not."

Kevin's face flushed. Rosemary had touched a nerve in him. She had attacked his way of helping people, and she had discredited his judgment of her. "What's with you?" he snapped. "All this business of not wanting to be part of something bigger than yourself."

Anger was rising in his voice. "If everyone in this world sat around and said, 'I want to do this all alone,' how many jobs would get done?"

Kevin looked squarely at Rosemary, his eyes blazing. "It's a cop out, that's what it is. You don't want to commit yourself to anything."

Turning to leave Rosemary, Kevin fired one last shot over his shoulder. "I've always seen you in a special way, Rosemary. From the very beginning. But now I see you've got this flaw—you only want to do things by yourself. You won't team up on anything."

He took a step, but stopped for an afterthought. "Nobody, not even you, Rosemary, nobody alone can be as effective as several people, maybe even two, working together."

Kevin stalked off, leaving Rosemary to ponder what she'd got herself into. How had a pleasant conversation suddenly disintegrated into a public shouting match in the front hall of Glenn High School? And the other night, the same thing with Grandpa. What's happening to my nerves, she wondered.

Kevin's words kept coming back to Rosemary as she sat through her morning classes . . . I've always seen you in a special way, but now . . . That's what he said. I've always, but . . .

Rosemary sincerely regretted having blown up. Looking back, she knew it was uncalled for. She was sorry she had publicly embarrassed Kevin, and herself. And even more, she hated having created a barrier between herself and Kevin.

At noontime Rosemary met Jackson and Shirley at their lockers, as planned. She looked around nervously for Kevin.

"Kevin cannot meet us," Jackson told her.

"Did you see him?" Rosemary asked.

"Yes."

"When?"

Jackson looked at his watch. "Ten minutes before."

"Was he mad?"

Jackson pulled out his dictionary to look up the word. "No. Not mad." He gestured to indicate foaming at the mouth.

"Angry, Jackson. Was Kevin angry?"

"Maybe he was angry," Jackson decided.

"It figures."

"Figures?" Jackson opened his dictionary.

"Forget it, Jackson. I wasn't very nice to Kevin this morning, and I'm sorry about it. Let's go and get some lunch."

Shirley closed her locker, but kept out two spiral-bound notebooks. Jackson took his book, explaining to Rosemary, "For writing new words."

"All right," Rosemary responded, "let's begin now." She wrote in Shirley's book, "We are going to eat in the cafeteria," saying the words slowly as she wrote them. Then she waited for Shirley and Jackson to repeat the sentence.

Rosemary led the Lees all over the building on the way to the cafeteria, writing sentences about everything they saw and did. Shirley and Jackson practiced saying the sentences as they walked, their eyes sparkling as they gained confidence.

"We're going to have you speaking fluent English in no time," Rosemary commented after several pages had been filled in the notebooks.

"I wish so!" Shirley said fervently.

They had reviewed the names of foods. They had written sentences about the equipment, the people, the sounds and colors in the cafeteria, and the Lees had said words over and over until they had them perfect. They had eaten and it was time for the bell, and all three of them were tired, but elated by their success.

Rosemary had kept an eye out for Kevin, figuring he probably would show up somewhere in the cafeteria, but he was nowhere in sight.

Kevin wasn't around when Rosemary walked home, either. She kept expecting to hear "Hey, Rosie," and Kevin's footsteps coming behind her as he caught up. But the sounds were only in her mind.

As Rosemary turned onto Muirwood Way, she felt uncomfortable having to pass Kevin's house. He might be inside, watching me walk by, she thought. Ducking her head, she self-consciously scurried past.

Rosemary wasn't sure exactly what she was uncomfortable about, or perhaps she didn't want to spell it out to herself. Deep in her heart she had to admit that Kevin was telling it straight. She did like to do things alone. What was wrong with that? It was her style. But she also had to agree grudgingly with Kevin that being alone wasn't always the best way to go.

What bothered Rosemary more was Kevin's unexpected confession. All in one brief moment, he had blurted out what Rosemary had only vaguely sensed for years. "I've always seen you in a special way, Rosemary." That kind of admiration was unsettling enough, but the next four words were the really bad ones. "But now I see . . ." Rosemary winced. That one hurt.

The thoughts of herself were soon overshadowed by thoughts of Della. Rosemary, approaching her house, nervously wondered what turn her grandmother had taken during the day.

"I'm home," Rosemary called to the empty house. She dropped her books on the couch and looked around to see if Arthur had left any messages. Finding none, she made the rounds of the rooms. Arthur's bed was made. The cinnamon rolls were gone. The sink was clean. Rosemary let out a sigh of relief. No signs of crisis. Arthur had apparently left for the hospital in an orderly fashion.

Knowing that the afternoon hospital visit would be hard on her grandfather, Rosemary began to fix dinner for him, listening all the while for the sound of his car pulling into the driveway.

With the dinner cooking, Rosemary wandered into the living room. She studied a couple of magazine covers, glanced at the evening headlines, and then stood at the window, feeling too restless to sit down. Her mind drifted down the block, stopped for a moment at Kevin's house and moved on to the room in Mercy Hospital where Arthur would be sitting quietly at Della's bedside. Remembering how fragile and passive her grandmother had seemed the day before, Rosemary found it hard to feel hopeful. A knot was tightening in her stomach.

❧ Chapter 7 ❧

Rosemary was still at the window, her eyes focused on some distant scene, when Arthur's car came into sight. Her eyes followed it down the street, bringing her mind back to 300 Muirwood Way.

Arthur stopped at the curb and sat motionless for a moment behind the wheel. At last, slowly and with effort he pulled himself out of the car, his face drawn and tense. Rosemary was struck with how old he suddenly seemed. She hurried to open the door for him.

"Are you okay?" she asked as he entered the house.

"Numb, Rosemary . . . just numb." Arthur paused and studied his granddaughter's face, unsure of how to go on.

"How's Gram?" Rosemary already sensed that the news was bad.

"She's gone, Rosemary." Arthur's words came out slowly,

his voice husky. ". . . couple of small attacks during the night . . . never regained consciousness . . . her heart simply stopped beating."

Arthur stared blankly at Rosemary, trying to grasp the meaning of his own words. ". . . heart simply stopped beating . . . stopped beating . . . stopped beating." He dropped onto the couch and wept softly.

A curtain of silence fell between the two surviving Magnusons. Rosemary, unused to seeing her grandfather cry, felt useless. Then her own sense of loss began to grow. She dashed to her room and flopped on the bed, her heart pounding, her cheeks burning. Over and over, her eyes mindlessly traced the patterns on the ceiling.

After a while, Rosemary stood up, took a jacket from the closet, and walked out the front door. Zombie-like, she passed her grandfather, still slumped on the couch. She saw nothing, heard nothing, thought nothing. Something inside said walk, so Rosemary walked. Down to the end of Muirwood, the full length of Hawthorne, around Crown Circle, and finally back to Muirwood.

Without knowing why, she eventually found herself knocking on Kevin's front door. In the blur of the moment, the earlier tensions between them were forgotten. When Kevin opened the door, Rosemary just stood there, her eyes glazed, her mind out of focus.

"Rosemary?" Kevin sensed trouble. "Your grandmother?"

Rosemary nodded, silent. Kevin's arms opened protectively, and Rosemary fell into them.

Kevin reached over to close the door on the TV news in the living room and gently led Rosemary across the porch to the steps. He pulled her down beside him, and they sat in silence. After a while Rosemary spoke in a voice that even to her didn't sound like her own.

"What do you do when someone dies, Kevin?"

For a moment, time seemed to stop. At last Kevin spoke haltingly. "Well, you have to call a funeral home, and then you have to make some plans, and you have to call your relatives, and . . ." Kevin paused, lost in his own painful memories. "That's hard, making those calls. On every call we made about my dad, I had to do the talking when Mom broke down." He stopped at that point, not wanting to overwhelm Rosemary.

She stood up slowly. "Thanks, Kevin. See you."

"Want me to do any phoning?" Kevin asked her.

Rosemary shook her head.

"What can I do?" Kevin begged.

Rosemary shrugged her shoulders.

"But I want to help . . . I know how you're feeling." He followed her down the steps. "And I hate to tell you this . . ." Now he was talking to himself. ". . . but it'll hurt more next week than it does today . . . and in a month it'll hurt even more." Kevin breathed deeply to ease the pressure in his chest. "But you survive," he whispered under his breath. "You really do, Rosie. Trust me, you do."

Unhearing, Rosemary headed for home, her mind a blur. When she opened the front door, she found her grandfather sitting in the chair by the living room phone. He looked so pathetic that Rosemary quickly forgot her own anxieties in her concern over the frail old man.

"Want me to make some calls, Grandpa?"

"Well, I already called the Garden Funeral Home and Pastor Gruen. But I haven't been able to bring myself to call Sigrid. Do you want to make that call, Rosemary?"

"Sure, Grandpa." Rosemary was thankful to have a definite task to perform. Everything seemed so mixed up. It was like playing a game with no rules. She took the hall phone into her bedroom so she could be alone and wipe away a tear if she had to. Ten minutes later she was relaying her great-aunt's message to her grandfather.

"Aunt Sigrid says she'll be on the road by four in the morning and will arrive by seven. We're not to bother cooking breakfast—she wants to do it for us."

"Oh, no!" Arthur looked distressed. "I wasn't thinking clearly . . . should have waited until morning . . . don't like to have Sigrid driving the Midas Creek Road alone at night."

"She's always done it, Grandpa. It was her job. She went anywhere she was needed."

"Yes, but remember she's retired now. She's not a young woman anymore. Those forty years as a rural nurse took their toll on her health."

"Should I call her back, tell her to wait until tomorrow?"

"Wouldn't do any good, now that she knows. We're the only family she's ever had. Nothing could keep Sigrid from coming to us when there's been a death."

"Yeah, I got that feeling. She sprang to life the minute she heard."

"Sigrid's at her finest in emergencies. You know, her years in the mountains haven't made her very sophisticated . . ."

"That's sure true," Rosemary interrupted. "For a smart lady, she can sound very dumb, calling you Artie."

Arthur grinned. "You'll notice she only does that when she and I are alone. In public she scrupulously preserves my dignity."

Rosemary was still on the subject of Aunt Sigrid's annoying ways. "And why does she have to keep calling me Little Rosemary?"

Arthur was amused. "As I was saying when we got sidetracked, Sigrid's years in the country maybe haven't made her sophisticated, but they certainly have made her real. She may get on your nerves, in fact, she's sure to, but it will be because she's trying so hard to help."

"I know, Grandpa. I hate the way I get annoyed with her."

Arthur looked at his granddaughter affectionately.

"She does give out more advice than a young person wants, but that's because she never had children of her own. She doesn't know what bothers teenagers. So let's try to be patient on the little things and appreciate her for her fine qualities. She's a nice, warmhearted lady who loves us dearly."

Suddenly, Arthur was pulling himself together. "Let's make things look a little better before she gets here." He plumped up the pillows in his chair, wiped some dust off the nearby end table with his sleeve, straightened a pile of magazines, and then stood up to study his unshaven face in the mirror over the fireplace.

"Hmmn," he mused, "I guess I'd better shave before seven o'clock, in honor of Sigrid's arrival."

"And I guess maybe I'd better clean up my room," Rosemary added. The abrupt return to ordinary routine was helping relieve the numbness.

"Della left her sewing room in good shape." Arthur was planning out loud. "So there's a room ready for Sigrid." He had started moving around to tidy up the house. "Why don't you work on the bathroom, Rosemary, and I'll tackle the kitchen."

Doing the extra things to make the house presentable for a guest left Rosemary no time to think. She fell into bed, exhausted, at nine-thirty. It wasn't until the lights were out and the house was silent that a new feeling of emptiness began to engulf her. Up to that moment, the reality of the situation had been difficult to grasp—she hadn't actually seen her grandmother dead.

Suddenly the enormity of her loss hit Rosemary. "I need Gram," she wailed in the dark. "I need my grandma." Sobs welled up in waves, bursting in a deluge of tears that soaked the pillow. Shaking all over, Rosemary curled up into a ball and hid under the blankets. After a moment, her hand reached out and pulled Benjamin Bear under the covers. Clutching Benjamin, Rosemary retreated from the present to safer times, unaware that the door to her room was opening.

At first it was open just a crack, barely enough for Arthur's face to peer through the darkness. Then the opening grew wider until he was standing in Rosemary's room, listening to his granddaughter's troubled breathing. After a moment he heaved a deep sigh of his own, padded across the dark room and sat on the edge of Rosemary's bed. His hand felt its way along the blanket-covered shape until it found the only thing sticking out—the top of Rosemary's head. Gently he stroked his granddaughter's hair and murmured, "You still have a grandfather, Rosemary. The old man's not senile yet. We'll make it. . . . We'll make it. . . . We will."

Rosemary's breathing became quieter, broken by an occasional sniffle. Arthur found some tissues in the dark and laid a pile on the pillow by Rosemary's face. Finally he leaned down, kissed the damp forehead, and with a final tender pat, tiptoed out of the room, leaving the door ajar. Rosemary slipped off into the release of sleep.

ઌ Chapter 8 ଝ

The sounds of Aunt Sigrid's
early morning arrival reached Rosemary through a drowsy
haze . . . the car stopping at the curb . . . Arthur opening the
front door to greet his sister . . . the bags being carried into
Della's sewing room . . . the hushed voices in the hallway.
Rosemary looked at the clock and marveled at Aunt Sigrid's
precision. She had promised to be there by seven, and she was.
Fifteen minutes early.

Rosemary burrowed under the blankets, pulled a pillow over
her head, and dozed for a while, even though her uneasiness
about the day made real sleep impossible. Finally she decided
that doing something, even the wrong thing, was preferable to
doing nothing. She got up and put on her robe. She could hear
Sigrid and Arthur talking in the kitchen.

"Artie, think about it this way: after your pain softens, you're still going to have all those good years together in your memory, and Della was spared a long illness. She would have hated being dependent on others."

"You're right, I'm sure, Sig, but I'm too numb to think that way today. I do appreciate your coming, though. You'll have to excuse my unresponsiveness."

"Of course. It's to be expected."

Soon the aroma of fresh-baked Swedish coffee cake drifted back to Rosemary's room, encouraging her to brave the initial greetings.

Here goes, she thought wryly as she walked to the kitchen door and waited for Sigrid to turn around.

"Oh, there's our Little Rosemary." Sigrid wrapped her grandniece warmly in her arms. Rosemary gave Arthur a What-did-I-tell-you look, and he shot back his Be-patient-she's-nice glance.

"It's nice of you to come, Aunt Sigrid." Rosemary's sense of courtesy came to her rescue.

"I'll always be here whenever I'm needed, dear. You know that! And now, why don't you both try to eat some of this coffee cake? Then we can make some plans."

Arthur and Rosemary, tempted by Sigrid's baking, ate more than they thought they would.

"This coffee cake is lovely," Arthur told his sister. "And your coffee is always outstanding." He cleared his throat and became serious. "As for plans, Sigrid, I have an appointment at the funeral home at ten this morning."

"That's good planning. We'll get the painful details taken

care of first thing." Sigrid was nodding thoughtfully. "Perhaps you and I should go to make the arrangements, Arthur, and spare Little Rosemary the distress."

Rosemary rolled her eyes at Arthur.

"Sigrid, Little Rosemary is sixteen."

"I know that, Arthur." Sigrid's tone was reproachful. "Don't you think I know the age of my only grandniece? But it's so much harder to do these things when you're young."

"I need Rosemary's help with the decisions," Arthur said softly. "It's essential for her to be satisfied with the way things are done."

Sigrid turned to Rosemary and put a gentle hand on the girl's arm. "I keep being surprised at how much you grow up between my visits. Your grandfather's right, dear. He needs you with him."

Rosemary was beginning to think that maybe Sigrid had it straight. She wasn't at all sure she wanted to make decisions about burying her grandmother. She struggled to keep her voice steady.

"I'll go and get ready." Rosemary picked up her dishes and headed for the sink.

"And I'll tidy things here while you dress," Sigrid said. "That way we'll all be ready at the same time. Don't worry about those." She took the dishes from Rosemary's hands and gave her grandniece a smile.

Rosemary put a hand on Arthur's shoulder as she passed him, and he put his hand over hers in a silent reassurance. Then she went to her room and closed the door.

Alone in her room, Rosemary paused before the mirror and studied her face. The dark circles under her eyes looked worse than she thought. But she smiled, recalling that her grandfather felt she was adult enough to help make the decisions at the funeral home. In fact, he said he needed her help. Rosemary stood up a little straighter and spoke to the young woman in the mirror. "I guess you can handle things. Why not?"

In keeping with her mature image, Rosemary made an extra effort to leave her room in order for the day. She tucked in the corners of her bed in neat, military fashion. She arranged her teddy bears on top of the smooth bedspread in an orderly line. She put away the clothes that were lying around and closed all the dresser drawers. Carefully she chose a conservative skirt and blouse to wear, instead of her favorite jeans and T-shirt.

She wasn't doing all these things because she felt they were necessary. She was doing them so Aunt Sigrid would be impressed with the way Arthur and Della had raised their granddaughter. Rosemary took another look at the unfamiliar young woman in the mirror and surveyed the now-organized room. Such a perfect person, she chuckled. Don't worry, it won't last!

The ten o'clock appointment at the funeral parlor allowed Rosemary more time than she wanted. A gnawing sense of unfinished business was taking hold of her, a feeling that she was supposed to be doing something, but she didn't know what.

Rosemary's mind wandered away from her room and the house on Muirwood Way. It's first period right now, she thought. Mr. Hazeltine will be looking at my empty seat and sending my name to the attendance computer. Kevin sitting in Mrs. Lozada's class, copying the assignment off the board. . . . Jackson and Shirley—so many problems in moving to a new country. Grandpa and Aunt Sigrid must have gone through the same thing.

Earlier, Rosemary hadn't really made the comparison between the Magnusons, who now spoke perfect English, and the Lees, who would have to master a whole new language before their adult lives could begin. I should have asked Gram more about how she taught English to Grandpa when he was a young immigrant from Sweden, Rosemary mourned. The next thought brought a smile. They must have communicated somehow—they got married.

Rosemary found herself caught up in a little dialogue with Della. Yes, Gram, I'm helping those kids from Burma, like you thought I should, and I didn't even get to tell you about it. Rosemary was beset by an overpowering sense of loss, of having been cheated out of sharing with someone who would approve.

Rosemary's thoughts shifted back to Kevin. I wonder if he's seen Jackson and Shirley today. Has he told them about Gram? Will he come to the funeral service? When his father died, did he feel the way I'm feeling now? Could I phone him after school, maybe go over to his place? I wonder . . .

"Rosemary," Arthur called, "we should leave in ten minutes. Will you be ready?"

"I'm ready now, Grandpa."

When Rosemary stepped out of her room in her conservative

outfit, Arthur did a double take. An exclamation was forming on his lips, but he stopped short when Rosemary held up a cautionary finger and pointed to Aunt Sigrid's room.

"Well, Rosemary, I see you're your usual well-dressed self," Arthur said for his sister's benefit. He and Rosemary grinned at their little act.

Sigrid came out of her room, dressed in her dark coat, hat, and gloves. She looked at Rosemary with a compassionate smile.

"My, you look nice, dear. That's such a becoming color with your fresh, clear skin." She paused uncertainly. "Aren't you wearing a hat?"

"A hat?" Rosemary was at a loss. "Aunt Sigrid, I don't even own a hat."

"Oh . . ." Sigrid was mentally updating herself. "I've lost touch with the styles, I guess. I'd forgotten girls don't wear hats these days."

Arthur winked at Rosemary and held her blazer while she slipped her arms in. "Shall we go, ladies?"

Rosemary was amazed at how jovial she and her grandfather were being. Having to be on good behavior for their guest seemed to keep their attention off the problems at hand.

Inside the funeral home, however, the mood changed abruptly. While the funeral director went over the options with Arthur, Rosemary sat there wondering where her grandmother's body was. She recoiled completely as they were led into another room to select a casket. Feeling faint, she backed out into the hallway and sat down. She could hear the voices, but her mind blocked out the words.

When Arthur and Sigrid finally returned to the hallway, Arthur put an arm around Rosemary's shoulders and asked, "You okay?" It was a husky whisper.

"Yes . . . no . . . I guess so."

"Well, at least we're finished."

Rosemary sighed, and Sigrid gave her an encouraging look.

"Oh, just a moment, Mr. Magnuson," the funeral director said. "Let me get your wife's wedding ring from the safe."

Arthur sagged and dissolved as the band was placed in his trembling hand. He hurried out the door, his shoulders shaking with sobs. Rosemary and Sigrid followed some distance behind, walking slowly toward the car. Arthur opened the door and climbed into the back seat. Rosemary automatically pulled out her keys and took the driver's seat.

As she drove, Rosemary kept an anxious eye on the rearview mirror. Arthur, scrunched down in the corner, kept a handkerchief pressed to his eyes. Tears welled up and trickled down Rosemary's cheeks, soaking her carefully chosen conservative blouse.

Sigrid tried to start a conversation.

"My, you have such beautiful flowers around here. And this lovely sunshine."

"Please, Aunt Sigrid, we'd rather not talk now." Rosemary was surprised at how decisively she said it.

Sigrid folded her hands in her lap like a little girl who had been told to keep quiet. She kept her head turned to the side window all the rest of the way home.

Occasionally Rosemary had to blink hard in order to see to

drive. She brushed the trickle of tears away with her hand as they rolled down her cheeks.

"I'll fix us a bite of lunch," Sigrid said when they were getting out of the car in front of the house. She turned to Rosemary, the hurt still showing on her face. "If it's permissible for me to speak."

Rosemary put an arm around her great-aunt's shoulders. "I'm sorry. I don't know what I'm doing right now. I didn't mean to cut you off. We need your sunshine."

"Of course, I understand," Sigrid murmured. "I'll get us some lunch."

Rosemary went to her room and closed the door. She needed to be alone to sort things out in her head. Pulling the snapshot album from her drawer, she sprawled on the bed and thumbed through it, pausing on the page that showed the family tree. She had thought it might be comforting to go back to her roots, but instead, the photos turned into a parade of her losses. She repeated the names as they were printed below each photo and mentally added up the score. Grandpa and Grandma Herndon, dead before she was born. Charles Clark Herndon, her father, dead before she was a year old. Susan Magnuson Herndon, her mother, killed along with her father. Della and Arthur Magnuson, holding her outside the courthouse on the day the adoption papers were signed. Now Della was gone!

Rosemary slammed the album closed and pulled a pillow over her head. She couldn't deal with it. She curled up with Benjamin Bear and retreated into sleep, never knowing that Sigrid called her to lunch or that Arthur opened her door to see if she was all right.

When Rosemary awoke, it was three o'clock. She could hear Aunt Sigrid and Arthur talking in the living room.

"Now, let's plan what we're doing tomorrow, Arthur. There are so many things to be attended to."

"Like what, Sig? I purposely planned a simple closed-casket graveside service because that's what Della would have wanted. I've asked Pastor Gruen to read from the Bible and play one of Della's favorite old Swedish hymns on his flute. The flowers for the casket have been ordered. There are no invited guests. So what's to be done?"

There was a long pause.

"Well, I'd better get the house ready for your church friends, who are sure to drop by later in the day."

"That's not really necessary. None of them will be critical. They'll just drown us in a deluge of homemade food and offers of help."

"Then what can I do to help, for heaven's sake?" Sigrid's usually controlled voice was high and frantic. "I came here to be of service. Where are the things I can do for you?"

"Well, I would be very grateful if you'd take care of Della's clothing and toiletries. They would be painful for Rosemary and me to handle, and I know Rosemary won't want any of them. Just leave the jewelry and scarves for her, and she can decide later which of them she wants to keep."

"Of course." Sigrid's voice was calm again. "I'll start right away. Shall I decide how to dispose of everything?"

"Use your judgment. I really don't know what should be done."

Rosemary could hear her great-aunt start down the hall.

"And thank you, Sigrid," Arthur called after her.

"You're very welcome, Artie." Sigrid's tone was soft. "I need to be of use to you—not to get on your nerves, or Rosemary's."

"You're fine, Sigrid. We're just not at our best right now."

When Sigrid's footsteps had moved into the bedroom, Rosemary sneaked into the living room to talk to Arthur.

"You doing okay, Grandpa?" she whispered.

"I guess so, Rosemary. How about you?"

"I don't know. Okay, I guess." Rosemary paused. "Grandpa, would it be all right if I invited Kevin to the service?"

"Of course, please do."

"Thanks. I think he wants to be invited."

Arthur was nodding thoughtfully. "That may be true, but more than that, you need him there."

Rosemary was stunned at how squarely Arthur had hit the target. Bullseye! Rosemary hadn't even admitted it to herself, but it was true, very true. Somehow she did feel a deep need to have Kevin near during this ordeal.

"I'll go tell him, then."

Rosemary left the house quietly and headed for the Melero home. When Kevin answered her knock, he seemed surprised to see her.

"Rosemary! Come on in. I just got home from school. Sit down." Kevin pointed to the couch and dropped down beside her. "I was just going to come over to your place. I see your Aunt Sigrid's car is there. How's it going with her?"

"Okay. She's a nice lady—sort of from another world."

"She loves to talk. Isn't that hard on your grandfather right now?"

"It's keeping him going, I think. He doesn't let her bother him."

"And how about you—she getting on your nerves?"

"Sometimes. I keep wishing she were Gram, I guess." Rosemary looked at Kevin and put on a brighter tone. "I'm glad you were going to come over."

"Yeah, I was going to bring you this." Kevin reached for a potted African violet wrapped in clear plastic. "It's from Shirley and Jackson."

"From the Lees?"

"I told them what had happened, and I guess they went to the shopping center at lunchtime. They seemed to feel deeply about your loss."

"Grandparents are important in their culture. That was really nice of them." Rosemary fell silent, touched by the Lees' concern. She stared into the ruffled pink flowers.

After a while Kevin broke the silence. "Did you make plans for a service, Rosemary?"

"Yes, that's what I came to tell you. It'll be a private grave-side service at eleven on Thursday. Just Grandpa, Aunt Sigrid, the minister, and me. And you, too, Kevin." Rosemary stared nervously at her hands. "That is, if you want to come. You don't have to," she added hastily.

"I want to, Rosemary."

"I don't feel very brave about this," Rosemary confessed.

"She was your mother and grandmother all in one. It's okay to feel lost." Kevin put a hand over Rosemary's. "Believe me, it's okay."

Rosemary got up to leave, clutching her potted plant.

"I'll be at your place at about ten-thirty on Thursday. Is that early enough?" Kevin asked.

"Sure. That's fine."

"Want me to do anything for you in the meantime? You've got another whole day before the service."

"No, Kev. I just want to be alone."

"Well, let me know if you change your mind."

"Thanks."

Rosemary started out the door, carrying the violet plant, then turned back to Kevin. "I'm glad you're coming to the funeral, Kev."

"I'm glad you asked me," he replied softly. "You'll get through it okay."

"With a little help from my friend."

"We'll get through it together." Kevin impulsively took her face in his hands and kissed her cheek.

"We will," he repeated in a hoarse whisper.

Rosemary walked home slowly, dazed.

❧ Chapter 9 ❧

Before Rosemary even lifted her head from the pillow on Thursday, she knew it was a gray day. The drainpipe outside her window was dripping steadily. When she finally did raise her head, she could see the garden blanketed in a thick coastal fog, the colors muted and the leaves dripping.

This is it, Rosemary thought—have to get through the day somehow. She got up to go to the bathroom, intending to go back to bed and sleep some more, but, as she emerged from the bathroom, Aunt Sigrid was waiting in the hall with a wide-awake smile.

"I have a warm breakfast ready, dear. It will be good for you."

Aunt Sigrid's cheerfulness, combined with the idea that anything about the day might be good for her, set Rosemary's nerves on edge. "I don't think I can eat, Aunt Sigrid." She went back into her room and closed the door. In a few moments she heard a soft knock.

"May I come in?" Arthur whispered.

When Rosemary opened the door, her grandfather ducked in and closed it behind him.

"I know you don't feel like eating. Neither do I. But for the sake of Sigrid's pride, maybe we can at least go to the table and admire her meal."

Rosemary knew her grandfather was right. She followed him to the kitchen and sat down, feeling brittle and ready to break. Aunt Sigrid smothered them with kindness. As she served a lot of delicacies that would remain untouched, she did her thinking out loud.

"We want the funeral to be nice for Della's sake, so we'll look our best this morning."

Rosemary went out of control. "We certainly will, won't we!" she replied tartly. Her great-aunt's "we's" were always like sandpaper on her nerves.

Sigrid gave her grandniece a reproachful glance and continued with her statement. "So we'll select our most appropriate outfits."

"We'll select very carefully, yes, we will!" Rosemary couldn't seem to find the off switch to stop her mimicking voice. She wanted to avoid conflicts with Aunt Sigrid, but she couldn't stand it when her great-aunt talked that way.

Arthur shot a warning look at Rosemary. She immediately excused herself.

"I'm sorry, Aunt Sigrid. I've got to be alone."

Rosemary hurried to her room and closed the door. After a few minutes alone, she calmed down and began to think about what she would wear. In spite of Sigrid's annoying way of saying it, Rosemary had to agree with the message. She wanted to be appropriately dressed for the service.

Rosemary went to her closet and considered the possibilities. In her mind she could hear Della saying, "That blue crepe blouse would be nice with your velveteen blazer, dear—you always look so lovely in it." Sure, Gram, Rosemary agreed, anything you want. If the fog lifts by midmorning, that outfit will be fine. She laid the clothes on her bed and got out her good shoes. You always loved it when I dressed up, didn't you, Gram? And I didn't dress up any more than I had to, did I?

Rosemary left the clothes to be put on later and stayed in her room looking for ways to pass the time until the funeral. Her stomach felt terrible, and her nerves remained raw, ready to snap at anything.

At nine forty-five, Sigrid tapped gently on Rosemary's door. "Be sure your outfit isn't bright," she called through the closed door. Her voice mirrored a mounting tension. "And wear your heels, dear."

"That does it!" Rosemary muttered under her breath. She grabbed her good clothes off the bed and threw them in a heap on the closet floor. "Doesn't she think I have any taste of my own?" Caught up in an irrational fury, Rosemary rummaged madly through her drawers, tossing clothes over her shoulders. Finally she found the T-shirt she was looking for. Driven by perverse rebellion, she slipped into jeans and the T-shirt and stood defiantly before the mirror.

It was as if she were looking at someone else wearing the GO CLIMB A ROCK T-shirt that Della had bought at Yosemite two years earlier. "I'm ready," the girl in the mirror announced.

Rosemary stared in horror at the image. "What am I doing?"

Brought abruptly back to reality, she checked her watch. Ten o'clock. She glanced out the window. The fog was burning off. Kevin would be there in half an hour. Systematically, the real Rosemary began her transformation.

Out of the closet they came—the soft blue crepe blouse, the muted plaid wool skirt, the velveteen blazer, the dressy shoes. And this time, the pearl earrings and the opal ring Della had given her on her sixteenth birthday. Rosemary Magnuson was going to look terrific. Like the terrific granddaughter of terrific grandparents. Looking terrific without any outside advice, because her own terrific taste dictated it.

At ten minutes after ten, Rosemary emerged from her room and announced, "I'm ready." Without pausing for reactions, she headed for the garage. "Tell Kevin I'll be right back if he gets here before me, will you, Grandpa? I'm taking the car for fifteen minutes, okay?"

"Where are you going?" Aunt Sigrid asked nervously. "We have to leave at ten-forty, you know, dear."

"I know. I'll be right back." Rosemary left without further explanation. She went into the garage to get the car, but couldn't resist pausing on the other side of the door to hear the conversation in the kitchen.

"Why are you so calm?" she heard Sigrid asking Arthur. "Aren't you nervous about her leaving this near to funeral time?"

"Give her breathing room, Sigrid. She'll be back in time." Arthur's tone was mild and unruffled.

"How did you suddenly acquire all this wisdom, Arthur? I well remember how you used to have your go-arounds with Susan."

"Rosemary's a lot like her mother." Arthur's tone was soft. "So this time I know what to expect. It's called experience."

Rosemary loved being compared to the mother she never knew. She hurried to the car, whistling brightly, almost forgetting that her errand was not a happy one.

When she pulled up to the house at ten thirty-five, the team was lined up on the front walk, waiting. Arthur, Aunt Sigrid, and Kevin.

"I was so worried when you left . . . all alone . . . troubled . . . the time so close . . ."

"Sorry, Aunt Sigrid." Rosemary turned to Arthur. "I decided we needed red roses." She held up a florist's package. "I got one for each of us to place on the casket, but two for me because she was both mother and grandma to me."

Aunt Sigrid dove into her purse for her hankie. Kevin flashed Rosemary a quick, proud smile. And Arthur, his eyes misty, put an arm around his granddaughter's shoulders as they walked to Sigrid's car.

When the family arrived at the cemetery, Pastor Gruen was talking to the man from the funeral home. The gravesite was ready, with the casket in place for lowering later. Much to Rosemary's surprise, the grave was surrounded by beautiful flowers. Apparently Pastor Gruen had got word to Della's friends.

Rosemary clutched her roses as the minister read the words and offered the prayers. When the clear notes of his flute pierced the stillness, tears rolled off her cheeks and dripped on the roses.

And abruptly it was over, so quickly that Rosemary just stood there like one of the granite monuments, clutching the flowers. Arthur made the first move, taking his rose and placing it tenderly on the casket. Sigrid followed, then Kevin and Pastor Gruen. Finally, Rosemary placed each of her roses on the casket and stood there with her head bowed. After a while, Arthur shook hands quietly with Pastor Gruen and stepped over to place a trembling hand on Rosemary's shoulder. The two turned and walked together to the car, with Sigrid and Kevin following.

No one talked on the way home. In the back seat, Kevin put a comforting arm around Rosemary's shoulders. Arthur, in the front seat by Sigrid, sat like a statue. The plaintive melody of the flute lingered in everyone's mind.

Sigrid parked her car in front of the house and got out with Arthur, leaving Kevin and Rosemary alone in the back seat.

"Can I do anything for you over the weekend?" Kevin asked. "Want to talk, or go for a ride, or anything?"

"No, but thanks anyway. I want to be alone—need to think. I'll just go into hiding in my room, maybe go to church with them on Sunday. That would please Grandpa."

"Okay, but if you need anything . . ." Kevin's eyes said more than his words. "Want to stop by my house on the way to school Monday? You could use some company on your first day back."

"Sounds good. I'll do that. Thanks for coming to the service."

Rosemary watched Kevin as he walked toward his house. His hand automatically reached up to discipline his forelock.

"Give up, Kev," she murmured to herself as her eyes followed him. "You've been working on it for at least ten years. Know when you're licked." She chuckled to herself in a moment of welcome relief between the tension of the funeral and the pain that would follow.

Rosemary kept to herself for the rest of the day, the emptiness growing inside her. Everywhere she turned, there were reminders of her grandmother—things Della had done, presents she had given Rosemary, places where they had sat and talked, and half-finished projects that Della would never complete. By bedtime Rosemary was so totally drained that she just dropped on her bed and sank into deep, unbroken sleep.

The weekend passed as a blur. Arthur and Sigrid allowed Rosemary her private grief, checking now and then to see if she wanted to join them or to eat something.

Mostly, however, Rosemary just made the time pass somehow, feeling relieved that on Monday she would be going back to the familiar routine of school.

ꙗ Chapter 10 ꙗ

Rosemary awoke on Monday morning when the sun, streaming through her window, hit her bed. The warmth started at her feet and slowly moved upward. Her grip on Benjamin Bear gradually loosened until finally she lay there, relaxed, almost smiling, her pillow flooded with sunlight.

I made it, she told herself. I got through it. The funeral. The weekend. I guess what we do now is pick up where we left off and get on with life. Rosemary had some vague notion that the funeral was the last hurdle to be surmounted. After that, everything would be smooth running.

Her spirits buoyed by that thought, Rosemary dressed and went into the kitchen for breakfast. Aunt Sigrid again had prepared her specialty, Swedish coffee cake, which Rosemary praised and only picked at. At last she left for school, grateful that there was another world for her to go to, one that hadn't been touched by Della Magnuson's death.

As Rosemary walked down Muirwood Way toward the Melero home to pick up Kevin, her emotions swung from one extreme to another. She was glad Kevin had suggested that they walk to school together. On the first day back after the funeral, it would be comforting to be with someone who already knew what had happened and would require no explanation.

Rosemary's hand was poised to knock on the Melero front door when Kevin opened it.

"Hi, Rosemary! Be right with you." He disappeared into the hallway. "Have a good day at work," he called to his mother. Picking up his books he closed the front door behind him. They walked a full block in silence, neither knowing quite what to say.

"Was Thursday night terrible?" Kevin finally asked. He glanced briefly at Rosemary.

"I survived," she replied.

Kevin waited a while before he asked, "How long will your Aunt Sigrid be staying?"

"I don't know. We haven't talked about that."

"I think she's nice—friendly and easy to talk to."

"Yeah, Kev, she would be a perfect candidate for a Newcomers Service Club, wouldn't she? You should be doing your usual recruiting." Rosemary's remark carried the barbs of an earlier encounter, but Kevin let it pass and kept the conversation on safe ground until they reached the campus. Just as they stepped inside the building, Rosemary spotted Shirley halfway down the hall.

"See you, Kev. I want to thank Shirley for the plant." Rosemary dashed away from Kevin, calling, "Hey, Shirley."

Shirley, hearing her name, turned around and spotted Rosemary, weaving her way through the crowds.

"Hello, Rosemary." Shirley's eyes reflected a tenderness she was unable to express in English words. "You are . . . well?"

Rosemary made a gesture with her hand to indicate yes and no, maybe and maybe not.

"I wanted to thank you for the beautiful African violet."

Shirley was listening intently, but couldn't quite catch the words. "Say it again, please. What is the English name for that kind of plant?"

"It's an African violet," Rosemary told her.

"African violet," Shirley repeated. "Oh . . . African," she said with sudden recognition.

There was a moment of embarrassed silence. Neither knew quite where to pick up the conversation, when so much had happened in between.

"How is the grandfather?" Shirley asked hesitantly.

"All right, so far," Rosemary told her. "My Aunt Sigrid is still there with him."

Rosemary suddenly realized how much she had missed her new friend.

"Shirley, how would you like to go to the supermarket this afternoon and learn some new words?" Rosemary paused, waiting for Shirley's reaction. "Jackson can come too, if he wants," she added.

Shirley's eyes brightened. "Yes, I will come. Thank you."

"Will your mother worry? Should you phone and tell her you'll be late?"

"Mother does not worry. Always, I go to the library, after school."

"Great. I'll meet you at your locker."

"But Jackson cannot come. He maybe has job."

"Oh? Where's he working?"

"He does not yet work, but today he will know."

"Where's the job?"

"My uncle—he owns print and copy center on Lincoln Street. Uncle needs more worker—maybe Jackson." Shirley returned to her own interests. "I will meet you after school. With glad."

"Glad doesn't do there," Rosemary pointed out gently. "You could say 'I will gladly meet you,' or else, 'I will be glad to meet you.' "

Shirley made a notation in her spiral notebook.

"We'll have fun without Jackson," Rosemary said impulsively. "We'll talk girl talk."

Shirley giggled. "We talk girl talk."

With hurried good-byes, they both dashed off to beat the first period bell. Rosemary's commitment to Shirley provided something positive to think about throughout a long and unnerving day that made her wish her loss could be more private. By the end of seventh period, she was really looking forward to meeting her friend, who wouldn't ask all kinds of questions and get weepy with sympathy.

Shirley showed up at her locker promptly, and Rosemary wasted no time on preliminaries.

"Ready to learn some more English?"

"Yes. Supermarket English?"

"Right. That's the plan for today."

Shirley put all her belongings into her locker except her purse, notebook and pencil. "Ready to learn Supermarket English," she announced with a satisfied smile.

While they were walking the five blocks to the shopping square, Rosemary filled Shirley in on some local trivia and then shifted the focus.

"Now it's your turn to talk, Shirley. Tell me how you and Jackson got American names. You surely weren't called Shirley and Jackson in Burma, were you?"

"Oh no." Shirley was eager to share this bit of personal history. "My Burmese name is Lai Lai and Jackson's is Than Zaw Win, but those names are written in a different alphabet."

"I know." Rosemary nodded.

"Well, when we first arrived at an American government office, the lady said we needed names she could write in English. She was kind and pretty, so I asked her name. It was Shirley. I decide my American name to be Shirley. And Than Zaw Win looked out the office window—the street sign said Jackson Street. He decides to be Jackson."

Rosemary shook her head in dismay. "Talk about risky. You might just as easily have become Bruennhilde and Battery!"

They were laughing as they reached the shopping plaza, but immediately became businesslike as they stepped inside the supermarket. Rosemary had Shirley show her some of the items her family purchased regularly, and they discussed generic and brand names until Rosemary felt that Shirley had had enough. After forty-five minutes in the store, they passed through the checkstand, giggling, with a bag of tortilla chips to eat on the way home.

Nibbling on the chips, they strolled past the other stores, expressing their preferences among the merchandise displayed in the windows. When they came to the ice cream shop, Shirley paused wistfully at the window.

"When I go in the ice cream store," she said, "I see thirty-five ice creams on the sign. I know only chocolate and vanilla."

"And you're tired of chocolate and vanilla." Rosemary was sympathetic. "Come on, let's learn ice creams." Peering into the shop, Rosemary was surprised to find a young man from her English class working behind the counter. They had never spoken, since their seats were on opposite sides of the room, but Rosemary had formed an impression that he wasn't her type. He did smile a lot, though, so he might be helpful. She led the way up to the counter, which had a glass front so the customers could view all thirty-five flavors.

The young man with FRANK on his shirt came alive in the presence of the girls. "What'll you have, ladies?" His head bobbed and his ice cream scoop jiggled to some private beat.

"First we have to identify at least twenty-five flavors," Rosemary replied. Then, deciding that sounded too weird, she added, "It's a project we're doing—for a foods class."

"Bet you can't get past fifteen without me telling you the names of the rest," Frank boasted. "I'm the key man here."

Shirley's pencil was poised. Rosemary bravely started down the rows of thirty-five unlabeled tubs, correctly identifying all the standard flavors and six of the exotic ones. Finally she was stuck, with nineteen to go.

"See? Like I said, you need me." Frank smiled smugly. He began to tap each tub with his scoop and say the names, reveling in his chance to show off—Heavenly Hash, Pumpkin Custard, Watermelon Sherbet, German Chocolate Torte . . ."

Shirley wrote as fast as she could to keep up with him. Frank finished off number thirty-five with a tapping of his scoop on the chrome ice cream case. "So what'll it be, ladies?"

"Whattleitbee? Whattleitbee." Shirley was whispering the word to herself, enchanted with its sound.

"It means 'What are you choosing?'" Rosemary explained.

Shirley opened her purse to count her money, glanced at the price board, figured her bus fare, and looked up at Frank confidently. "Heavenly Hash, single scoop, please." She turned to Rosemary and giggled. "I don't remember which it is, but I like the name."

"Make it two," Rosemary added.

"Two, coming up," Frank said, winking at Rosemary.

He passed the cones over the counter with a well-rehearsed smile. "There you go. Come back again and try Marble Mint Mocha, our newest flavor. It's terrific—take my word for it."

"Thanks," Rosemary replied, thinking that Frank's word was not something she would want to follow on many things beyond ice cream.

"See you in English," he called as Rosemary and Shirley reached the door of the shop. "Hey, what's your name?"

Rosemary turned back to him, surprised. "It's Rosemary."

Her manner was guarded. "I didn't think you recognized me. I've only been there a few days this semester."

"You sit in the first row near the door," Frank replied with a sly wink. "Close to the door, for quick exits. I sit in the back corner. Way back, for watching girls."

"Yeah," Rosemary replied in a flat tone. She hurried out of the shop.

"I think Frank likes you," Shirley whispered.

"No, he doesn't. He just likes to practice his line on any girl that's around."

Clutching their napkin-wrapped cones, Rosemary and Shirley sauntered past the other stores. When they passed the yard goods shop, Rosemary paused to look in the window. "Do you like to sew, Shirley?"

"Yes. Very much. My mother sews well. She was a . . ." Shirley groped for the right word. "A lady who sews?"

"A seamstress."

"Yes, when we were in Hong Kong, in a very expensive shop."

"Great. Then you like yard goods shops, don't you?" Rosemary had found a soulmate.

"Yes, I buy too much, always, in cloth shop."

"So do I, Shirley, so do I. But let's do the store together some day, anyway. Want to?"

"Yes. Oh, yes!"

"It's getting late now," Rosemary said reluctantly. "We'd better get back to school before they lock up. We might not get our books from our lockers."

"Then, no homework."

They laughed and hurried back to the school.

With their books in their arms, they parted to go their separate ways. Shirley headed for the bus stop with new confidence in her walk. Rosemary suddenly sagged. Back to the other world. For over an hour she had almost forgotten.

ᓃ Chapter 11 ᕽ

As Rosemary turned toward home, she pulled her jacket closed. The fog bank that had hovered earlier above the ocean now drifted inland like a great gray carpet, unrolling over the hills and across the city. In a nervous gesture, Rosemary brushed her hair back from her face and tried not to think about things at home.

When she reached Muirwood Way, she wanted to turn and run, but her sense of responsibility made her go on. She approached the front door hesitantly and put her key in the lock, longing to hear her grandmother's voice calling "Welcome home, dear." Instead, she heard Arthur and Sigrid talking in the sewing room. Pausing at the open door, Rosemary listened.

". . . I simply know that you and Rosemary can't start to make your adjustments with a guest in the house, Arthur. You're both on good behavior for me, and you can't live that way. So I'm going to step out of the picture temporarily and let that lovely young grandniece of mine blossom into womanhood as she takes on new responsibilities."

"But, Sig . . ."

"No 'buts,' Artie. I'm packed, and as soon as Rosemary gets here I'll be on my way. I'll get to Orchard Valley before sunset and stay overnight with Tillie Golden, so you don't have to worry about Midas Creek Road in the dark."

"All right, Sig, I know there's no point in trying to tell you what to do."

"I love you both dearly, and I'll be back later for a good visit."

"We'll look forward to it. Here, I'll take your things to the car."

As Arthur and Sigrid stepped into the hallway, they saw Rosemary standing by the front door. Sigrid embraced her.

"Oh, I'm glad you're home. I'm ready to leave, dear, but I didn't want to go without telling you good-bye. Your grandpa will explain why I'm not staying longer. I'll be back again for a nice visit later."

This new turn of events took Rosemary by surprise. Although she had found many of Sigrid's habits irritating and often wished she weren't there, the thought of actually being without her was unnerving. Aunt Sigrid, with her practical cheerfulness and her zest for living, had been keeping things going in the household.

Sigrid held Rosemary at arm's length and studied her fondly. "I'm so proud of you!"

Bewildered by the unexpected wish fulfillment, Rosemary patted her great-aunt's back uncertainly. "We'll look forward to your next visit, Aunt Sigrid. Thanks for coming. You've been a big help." She reached for Sigrid's bag. "Here, I'll carry it." Rosemary was moving instinctively, still not fully grasping the reality of her great-aunt's departure.

She loaded Sigrid's belongings into the car, and Arthur protectively checked the oil, water, and tires. Sigrid climbed in and started the engine. As she was ready to release the brake and drive away, Rosemary suddenly shouted, "Wait, Aunt Sigrid, wait!" She dashed into the house and came racing back with something clutched in her hand. Reaching through the open window, she pinned Della's cameo brooch onto Sigrid's coat lapel.

"I want you to have it, Aunt Sigrid. Grandpa gave it to Gram on their twenty-fifth wedding anniversary."

Too choked up to respond, Sigrid nodded and patted Rosemary's hand. Then, blowing kisses as she pulled away, she drove off.

Rosemary and Arthur stood at the curb until the little car had disappeared from sight, before they silently walked together into the house.

Rosemary flopped on the couch in a way she wouldn't have thought of doing when her great-aunt was there.

"That was a lovely gesture, giving her Della's cameo brooch," Arthur said softly. He was seated in his armchair, studying his hands, slowly massaging his knuckles.

"I was afraid you'd be mad, Grandpa."

"It was yours. You were free to give it away if you wished. And Sigrid was deeply touched."

They lapsed into silence, retreating into their private

thoughts. Rosemary began to wonder what was going to happen with their meals, now that Sigrid was gone.

"You hungry?" she asked, hoping that Arthur would say that dinner was in the oven. Instead, Arthur shook his head.

"I don't feel interested in food tonight, Rosemary. You just eat whatever you want."

"I'll fix a little something for you, Grandpa. You need to eat. And you want the TV on, don't you?"

"No."

"More light, at least?"

"No."

Rosemary went to the kitchen and discovered that Sigrid had left two dinners ready to be warmed. She poured some milk, heated the food, and took the trays to the living room to eat with Arthur.

Instead of the man who had responded warmly to Sigrid's attempts at cheerful conversation, Rosemary suddenly found herself with a grandfather who had become withdrawn and remote. Experiencing an unexpected letdown herself, she had no resources for cheering up someone else. She finished eating and, finding it too gloomy in the dim living room with no TV and no talk, went to her room.

When it became dark, Arthur headed for his room, too, saying a brief good-night and closing his door. Without the optimistic influence of Aunt Sigrid to buoy her up, Rosemary slipped morosely into a case of self-pity. What's it going to be from now on—a do-it-yourself breakfast, do-it-yourself dinner, do-it-yourself laundry, do-it-yourself entertainment? Do-it-yourself everything? Wonderful!

Actually, Rosemary was perfectly capable of doing any of those things for herself. She had done all of them many times. Della hadn't let her grow up helpless. It wasn't really the do-it-yourself that was troubling her, it was a gnawing sense of panic that all in one day she was being forced to become totally responsible for herself—no test runs, no easing into it, no transition time. Alone in her room, Rosemary spent a dismal evening with these mushrooming fears, unaware of the depth of her grandfather's own desolation.

By nine o'clock Arthur was asleep and the house had grown dark. Rosemary could have turned on lights in every room, but her mind was too paralyzed to do anything besides passively accept things as they were. It's like a tomb, she thought grimly —silent, dark, sealed off from the world of the living. Is this what's ahead? She shuddered. Night after night of this?

Rosemary moved to the living room. One dim little lamp was on, just as Arthur had left it. She tried watching TV, but it only increased her sense of isolation. Everyone on the screen was animated, making her recall how she used to chat with Della in the sewing room, or laugh with Arthur over a TV comedy and later have hot cocoa with both of them at bedtime.

Finally, Rosemary reached for the phone and idly dialed Kevin's number. She hadn't given much thought to why she was calling him or what she expected from him. She just sensed that hearing his voice would put her in contact with the world of the living.

"Kevin? . . . Hi . . . Oh, just sitting in the living room . . . alone . . . Grandpa's asleep . . . dead to the world . . . he went to bed early, right when it got dark . . . Yeah, Aunt Sigrid went back to Midas Creek . . . No one's here . . . except me . . . and it's so boring, all alone . . . No, oh no, Kev, I didn't mean that . . . You're probably doing your homework, or something . . . You don't need to . . . Are you sure? . . . Well, okay . . . if you want to . . ."

Rosemary hung up with a terrible feeling about the whole thing. I'm using Kevin, she thought with horror. I don't particularly want to see him right now. It's just that being this much alone is getting to me.

Oh well. Rosemary shrugged off her misgivings. He wanted to come.

A few minutes later, there was a soft tap on the door. When Rosemary opened it, Kevin was smiling shyly. His hair was recently combed and still staying in place. He was wearing one of his best looking plaid shirts, and he had a glow about him that Rosemary hadn't seen before.

"Hi, Kev. Come on in."

"I'm glad you called me, Rosemary."

"Thanks for coming."

After the formalities, there was an uncomfortable moment of silence. Now that she had him there, Rosemary began to wonder what she had had in mind when she called him.

Kevin had been alone with Rosemary countless times during their years of growing up together, but never in this kind of setting—a softly-lighted living room, no one else likely to appear for hours, and a special invitation from Rosemary to come over. While Rosemary had stirrings of doubt, the picture was perfectly clear to Kevin. He took off his jacket and sat down next to Rosemary on the couch.

"Well," he said chattily, "how did today go?" He stretched his arm and laid it along the back of the couch.

"Too many people at school had to tell me how sorry they were about Gram."

"Yeah, I know." Kevin's arm slid along the couch until it was right above Rosemary's shoulders. "The sympathy is hard to take." He put his arm around Rosemary. "Did I see you going off with Shirley after school?" Kevin gently pulled Rosemary closer to him.

"Uh huh, we went to the shopping center to learn Supermarket English."

"Great." Kevin pressed lightly on Rosemary's head until it rested comfortably on his shoulder. She began to relax, enjoying the security of feeling like a little girl again, protected.

"We went to the ice cream shop, too," she continued. "This guy Frank, who works there, told us the names of all thirty-five flavors, and Shirley wrote down every single one."

Kevin chuckled at the idea, then began to stroke Rosemary's arm. A warm tingle ran down her spine, and she snuggled closer.

"Shirley had never ordered anything except chocolate and vanilla before . . ." Rosemary began talking faster and faster as Kevin's other arm crossed over her chest. "We both ordered Heavenly Hash . . ."

Kevin's body followed his arm across her until his cheek was pressed against Rosemary's. His mouth was nearing hers.

"Kevin," Rosemary whispered tentatively.

"Hmmn?"

"Kevin?" she said in a questioning tone.

"Rosie . . ."

"Kevin!" she shouted just before his lips touched hers. "That's not what I want!" She shoved him away.

Kevin reeled back, his cheeks flushed. "What's with you?" he asked gruffly. "What's this all about? You send out signals and then you cancel them, just like that?"

"I didn't send out signals. What are you talking about?" Rosemary was defensive.

"Oh, cut it out, Rosemary!" There was annoyance in Kevin's voice. "You're not a baby, after all. You phone a guy and tell him you're all alone and lonesome. The guy comes to your place. There's no one around, and you're in an almost dark living room sitting on the couch. That's not sending signals? Come on!"

Kevin was shoving his arms into his jacket. "And besides, I wasn't forcing anything on you, Rosemary. You were right in there with me, liking it."

Rosemary was at a loss to explain her mixed-up feelings. "I didn't have any idea . . . I never thought . . . when I called you . . . I wasn't thinking at all, Kevin, I swear."

"Well, you'd better start thinking, Rosemary. I'm telling you, that's not a game you can cancel at half time with very many guys. I'm surprised you could act so dumb when you're not."

Kevin started to leave, but turned back to fire one more shot. "There aren't very many guys who are going to care enough about you to stop!"

Kevin stalked out the door, leaving Rosemary stunned, asking herself how she had ever bumbled her way into such a situation. She turned off the dim little lamp, groped her way down the hall, and flopped on her bed, drained, wondering if she and Kevin could ever get back to their relaxed and comfortable childhood friendship after such an awful setback.

In the darkness, Rosemary's mixed up feelings passed before her in a confused parade . . . blew it . . . ruined everything . . . hurt my best friend. Can we ever be the same . . . be the same again? Is that what I want . . . be the same? A nagging doubt had crept into the parade . . . is our old childhood friendship what I really want back? Too tired to think . . . later . . . somehow figure it all out . . . later.

ঌ Chapter 12 ঌ

When morning came, Rosemary resisted the dawn. As the sun's rays broke through the fog to spread across her bed, she burrowed deeper under the blankets, trying to hold back the new day. But, when she considered what staying at home would be like, she threw the covers off and got out of bed, glad it was a school day. Any problems at school would be modest by comparison with last night's.

Rosemary showered and dressed for school, made her bed, and headed for the kitchen, hoping her grandfather would get up and join her for breakfast. But there was no sound from Arthur's room, so she went ahead and fixed her own breakfast and sat down to eat it alone. As she swallowed her dry cereal and toast, she reviewed the changes in her life.

Never knew my parents. Gram's gone. Looks as if I'm losing

Grandpa, too, and now the situation with Kevin. I'm losing everyone!

Since Arthur's door was still closed when she finished breakfast, Rosemary left a good-bye note in the kitchen and closed the front door quietly. She was beset by doubts. What am I going to school for when I'm such a mess? I can't concentrate on anything. Is this what I'm going to be like from now on?

She started down the first step and almost lost her nerve. What if I meet Kevin? she thought in panic. What on earth do I do if I meet Kevin?

Rosemary gave the blooming chrysanthemums a friendly tap, causing a shower of dew to splash to the ground. Then she cut across the lawn, leaving behind a trail of footprints on the damp grass. The fog must have been thick last night, she thought as she shook the water off her shoes. It's going to take a while for the sun to dry things out today.

Rosemary wondered if foggy mornings were always going to remind her of the day of Della's funeral. Was it only a few days ago? Time was blurred, but her memory of the pain was crystal clear.

Poor Kev . . . Rosemary started thinking about their misunderstanding. He's right, she had to admit. Not many guys would care enough about me to put up with my moods. How will I face him now? she wondered with embarrassment. Approaching Kevin's place, she looked around warily to see if he was anywhere in sight, then walked briskly past his house, eyes straight ahead.

As Rosemary entered the school she caught a glimpse of him.

A second later she did a double take to confirm what she thought she had seen. It was true. Kevin was walking down the hall with a beautiful dark-haired girl, and obviously he was enjoying himself. He was smiling and carrying on an animated conversation, while she laughed lightly. Rosemary stared at the couple as they disappeared in the hallway crowd.

All morning long she kept rolling the scene over in her mind. Many times before she had watched with mild interest as Kevin had shown new students around the school. Most of them were shy and nervous in their new surroundings, but this young woman didn't seem the least bit in need of orientation. She was perfectly dressed and completely self-assured. Rosemary looked down at her own clothes and felt less than devastating.

When fifth period came, Rosemary hurried around to Shirley's and Jackson's lockers, eager to have lunch with her new friends.

"Hello, Rosemary," Shirley said with a warm smile. "I am glad to see you. I don't think Kevin will eat with us."

"How do you know?" Rosemary was dying for some news, but tried to sound disinterested. "Did you see him, Shirley?"

"Yes, he walked past here."

"Did he stop and talk?"

"Yes, he introduced me to another newcomer. She's from Boston, I think he said."

"Was she dark-haired, little, about so tall?"

Shirley nodded. "And very beautiful. Kevin was going to show her where the cafeteria is."

"Naturally!" Rosemary retorted wryly.

Shirley studied Rosemary's face for a clue. "I thought Kevin was your boyfriend—no?"

Rosemary was shocked by Shirley's observation. "Oh no, Shirley. We're just old friends from way back."

"Oh, then you don't care if he has lunch with Yvette."

"Why would I care?" Rosemary shrugged off the idea. "Is that her name? Yvette?" She tried not to appear hungry for details. "Yvette?"

"I think you care," Shirley said. "I see the way you look."

"You see a lot, don't you?" Rosemary grinned at Shirley and changed the subject. "Where's Jackson?"

"He changed his classes. Now he goes to a class for fifth period. No more of lunch. He goes to the job at the seventh period."

"You mean he has six straight classes and then goes to work?" Rosemary asked incredulously.

"Straight classes. What is a straight class?"

"Six in a row, I mean." Rosemary gestured to explain it.

"Yes, that's right." Shirley looked at Rosemary with sadness in her eyes. "And I cannot go with you again to the shopping center, and yard goods shop, and ice cream shop. I have the job with Uncle, too, now."

"What?" The bottom was dropping out of Rosemary's world. "When do you start?"

"Four o'clock."

"Today?"

"Yes, four to nine."

"Every day?"

"Not Sunday."

"We were going to have fun after school." Rosemary's disappointment was becoming another personal loss.

"I like doing things with you—I am sad about that," Shirley said. "But it is good I can earn money for my family. I must help the family."

"It's going to be hard on your homework," Rosemary pointed out.

"I will do the homework, too. I will sleep not so much."

"I've got to hand it to you, Shirley."

Shirley stared at Rosemany, totally mystified. She flipped the pages of her dictionary, then looked up, still puzzled. "I don't know what to look up."

Rosemary laughed. "The expression 'I've got to hand it to you' means, I must compliment you. I must say you are brave."

"Brave?" Shirley looked up brave and understood. "But getting a job is not a very brave thing. In my family we all must work to start in America."

"You've got everything straight, Shirley." Rosemary's comment was wistful. "I wish I had."

The fun was gone from their lunch-hour conversation. Rosemary conscientiously pointed out new things, but her mind was elsewhere. Shirley learned words in a businesslike way, but her heart wasn't in it. When the lunch hour came to an end, Rosemary could feel herself coming apart.

"Well, good luck on the job," she told Shirley, as if they were parting forever. In her upset state of mind, it never occurred to Rosemary that they could continue to meet at lunch-time. Her sense of loss was so acute that she could only see Shirley as one more person leaving her.

All through sixth and seventh periods Rosemary nursed her disappointment about no more after-school excursions with her friend. When school finally closed, she felt incredibly lonely.

She walked home slowly, her feet dragging and her thoughts turned inward. No Shirley, no Jackson. I've lost two more people, she mourned. Gram and Kevin and Grandpa and now the Lees. I don't care what Kevin says, there's only one way to go—alone. Look what happens when you care for people—you just lose them. Alone is the only way. Anything else is too risky. Too risky, she repeated to herself. Just too risky.

Reluctantly, Rosemary turned into Muirwood Way, wishing there were someplace else she could go. The hours until bed-time looked endless. Maybe I'll change to my running clothes and go for a long, long run, she thought. Run away for a while.

When Rosemary opened the front door, she knew instantly that she was in for another evening of silence. Arthur, still unshaven, was in the same chair.

"Hi, Grandpa."

"Hello, Rosemary."

"Have you been there all day?"

"Most of it, I guess."

"Why don't you turn on the TV?"

"It doesn't interest me much anymore."

This time Rosemary didn't ask about dinner. She put her

jacket in her room and, with some resentment, went to the kitchen. There were no signs that Arthur had eaten at all during the day. Rosemary took one of the church women's casseroles from the freezer, put it in the oven, and went to her room to wait for it to bake. She couldn't think of a thing she wanted to do. Sitting idly on her bed, she rejected one idea after another. Boring, waste of time, too much effort. She went back to the kitchen to watch the oven timer until the bell finally rang. Then she slapped some of the casserole onto two plates and poured two glasses of milk. Sloppy, so what! It's not my job to be the cook and feed us, she thought, somewhat irrationally.

"Here." Rosemary shoved a plate and glass at Arthur.

"Thank you, Rosemary," Arthur gently replied as he accepted the food.

Rosemary went back to the kitchen for her own plate and sat down to eat near the TV. This time she didn't ask Arthur if he wanted it on. She just turned it on. She was going to go crazy without some noise in the house.

"Don't you have homework?" Arthur asked after a while. "School started ten days ago, and I haven't yet seen you studying. I'm afraid you're going to fall so far behind that you can't catch up."

"A few things have happened, you know!" Rosemary snapped.

The minute she said it, she hated herself. A look of pain crossed Arthur's face, and Rosemary began to ache inside.

"I'm sorry I sounded like that, Grandpa." Rosemary's eyes

were misty with tears. "I know you're right about my school-work, but I just can't seem to concentrate. I can't get myself to do anything right."

"Neither can I, Rosemary," Arthur confided. "And I'm really trying, too."

Arthur's meal remained untouched in front of him as he and Rosemary stared silently at the TV screen. Unable to fill each other's overwhelming needs, they retreated into their separate rooms at bedtime with cursory goodnights.

Thus a pattern was established in the Magnuson household. All the days and all the evenings began to seem alike, as if stamped out with a cookie cutter. They blended into one another with no separate identities. For two weeks Rosemary moved through the blur with little sense of passing days, until she suddenly had the strange feeling that she was caught up in a time warp, replaying some earlier scene.

One day she put the key in the front door lock and pushed the door open. I'll bet he hasn't moved, she thought. Watch, he'll still be in that chair. Rosemary's prediction was grimly accurate. Sure enough, Arthur was sitting in his chair, his face a mask. His hair was tousled, his stubble was becoming a white beard, and his clothes were wrinkled. It was a scene so familiar that Rosemary had it memorized. I don't believe it, she thought with alarm. I'm going around in an endless circle.

I can't deal with him, she groaned to herself. I have too many problems of my own. It never occurred to her that Arthur's loneliness might be even more crushing.

"Hi," she mumbled as she passed him.

"Good evening, Rosemary," Arthur replied. His voice was weak, but still dignified.

"Have you done anything today?" Rosemary asked, her voice taking on an accusing tone.

Arthur shook his head slowly.

"Okay," Rosemary said grudgingly. "I'll get you some dinner."

The food supplies in the kitchen were almost exhausted and Rosemary had trouble finding much of anything to eat. She threw together some leftovers, divided the food between two plates, and took one to Arthur.

As she ate, Rosemary toyed with the idea of going to the market for supplies, but some strange resentment held her back. Why should that be my job, she argued. I go to school all day. Grandpa has lots of time. He should be able to handle such things.

Rosemary even rejected the idea of running. Forget it, she decided. What good would it do anyhow? What good is anything anymore?

And so the two despondent Magnusons descended into an emotional stalemate.

❧ Chapter 13 ❧

Rosemary awoke the next morning feeling ill. Can't go to school like this, she thought—head aches, stomach feels terrible, couldn't possibly sit through six classes. She reached for Benjamin Bear and hugged him tightly. He had seen her through all her childhood illnesses. "What'll I do, Benj?" she whispered into the fur ear. ". . . need to stay curled up in bed today. I can't face anything more."

Memories of the times when she had stayed home with bronchitis were vivid in Rosemary's mind—Della hovering over her, feeling her forehead, urging her to drink a little more juice, bringing some sewing in so she could sit by the bed. And when Rosemary was well, Della always found it difficult to get her out of bed and back to school.

"Who will ever take care of me again, Benj?" Tears rolled

down Rosemary's cheeks and soaked into the pillow. She sobbed quietly for a while.

When the sobbing subsided, Rosemary began to consider her options. Staying home from school would mean taking care of Grandpa for eight more hours. A school day can't be worse than a full day at home, with this dark, closed-in feeling, she concluded. She propped Benjamin up against the headboard and dressed for school, never pausing to wonder if the house might be having the same effect on her grandfather. In Rosemary's irrational thinking, Arthur was the cause of the gloomy situation rather than a victim.

With Arthur still asleep, Rosemary gulped down a quick breakfast and took off for school, her only plan being to get away, simply to get away.

She had walked a few blocks when she suddenly started to laugh. What's the matter with me? School isn't away. Away is the ridge trail. I should know that by now, after all the problems I've worked through up there, alone with my thoughts. At the next corner, Rosemary turned west instead of east and headed for the coast, making the decision to cut school for the day without the slightest twinge of conscience and without any worry about Arthur or the school. Her one goal was to get away.

It was a perfect day for escaping. The morning fog was burning off early, and Rosemary could tell it was going to be pleasantly warm. Pleasant. That's a nice change, she thought. Nothing has been pleasant for a while. As she passed the last group of homes and started across the open grassy hilltop, she raised her eyes to the sky and took a deep breath. Good medicine, she thought. A day up here could help more than a day in bed.

Rosemary followed the trail, walking slowly, the way she had often walked with Della. Moving slowly allowed her attention to focus on the miniature world around her—a few off-season wildflowers, birds of many kinds, the sounds of insects, an occasional lizard, wild grasses—all the things Della had taught her to recognize and respect.

After a while she wandered away from the trail and down the side of a hill, until she found a secluded spot, away from the joggers, where she could be alone in the middle of the small world. Gazing out to sea with the sun warming her back and the ocean breeze cooling her face, Rosemary's mind began to uncoil and drift back in time: Della showing her a hidden world in nature, Della identifying bird calls for her, Della pointing out the shadings in the ocean, Della making a small girl feel like part owner of a remarkable world. "By being aware of its existence, you own part of the world of nature, Rosemary." This is what Della had taught her. "And no one can take these riches away from you," she used to say. "They're yours, Rosemary. Yours." Della's voice was so clear in her mind that Rosemary lay back on the grassy slope and listened.

As she listened, her mind floated free, swirling around in time. Images paraded past her in a loose procession—quick glimpses of long-forgotten moments, sixteen years of living. As Rosemary dropped in and out of consciousness, her resentment and pain were gradually giving way to a vague realization that maybe everything wasn't gone, that maybe Della's legacy had been to teach her how to live. With the beginnings of peace taking hold within her, Rosemary slipped into a quiet sleep.

When she awakened, the angle of the sun had changed. She looked at her watch. Two o'clock? She felt her face. Too much sun. But, to her surprise, when she stood up and stretched, she somehow felt better. I feel alive, she marveled. I thought I might feel dead forever.

Rosemary wandered on down the ridge for an hour, unwilling to leave the spell the trail was casting on her. At three o'clock, however, reality intruded. Maybe if I get home at the regular time, Grandpa won't know I cut, she figured. Maybe, just maybe, the attendance office didn't even phone him. With that hope, Rosemary turned around and tramped back into the other world.

As each step brought her closer to the house on Muirwood Way, where the sun refused to shine, the mellowness of the day receded. Rosemary had begun to come alive in the sun and wind, and she hated having that feeling fade away.

On the doorstep, she held back a moment, reluctant to abandon her aliveness. Well, here goes, she decided as she put the key in the lock. Guess where Grandpa will be sitting. She pushed the door open. The chair was empty.

"Grandpa?" she called.

Hmmn, maybe the kitchen? The garden? The bathroom? Taking a nap, maybe? Rosemary moved through the house.

"Hey, Gramp, I'm home."

When she found her grandfather in the bedroom taking a nap, Rosemary felt relieved. For a moment she had been gripped by panic. Sure, a nap, she thought with unexpected tenderness. Why not? The old man looked so frail and vulnerable that Rosemary decided she had better put one of the casseroles in the oven so there would be something nourishing for him to eat when he woke up.

Rosemary backed quietly out of the doorway, feeling a touch of guilt about the way she had been treating her grandfather. She decided to make dinner a little better, for a change. Maybe even go to the market after the meal.

While the casserole baked, Rosemary set the table decently for the first time in days, even putting out paper napkins instead of her recent paper towels. When she finally put the dinner on the plate, she was proud of her efforts. Grandpa will be surprised, she thought. Maybe he'll even perk up a little bit. Rosemary went to the bedroom door.

"Dinner's ready, Grandpa."

Arthur didn't stir.

"Grandpa—hey, want some dinner?"

Seeing no movement, Rosemary stepped closer.

"Gramp!"

Rosemary went over to Arthur and shook his shoulder, but there was no response. For an instant, the thought flashed through her mind that her grandfather might be dead, but when she looked closely she could see that Arthur was breathing and his color was okay. Rosemary studied the sleeping form, debating whether she should rouse him for dinner or let him sleep till morning. It began to dawn on her that Arthur's breathing was much too slow.

"Grandpa, wake up for dinner!"

Rosemary shook her grandfather's shoulders hard, then tried to lift him to a sitting position. The body was limp in her arms. And then she spotted a pill bottle where Arthur's hand had been. Open . . . empty. The body flopped back onto the bed as Rosemary clapped a hand over her mouth.

"Oh, God! Gram's sleeping pills!"

She grabbed the bottle and read the label. "Della Magnuson. Take as directed. Chloral Hydrate 500 mg."

"What do I do? Who should I call?" she shouted to the empty house. When she grabbed the phone, she saw a smudged emergency number that Della had stuck on it long ago. Frantically, she dialed the number.

"My grandfather's unconscious!" she shouted at the voice on the other end. "He's taken a bottle of sleeping pills!"

Rosemary tried to steady her breathing while she waited for her call to be transferred. The paramedics answered quickly.

"The bottle's empty," she replied to their questioning. "It says Chloral Hydrate 500 mg . . . I don't know how many were in it . . . Yes, he's breathing . . . No, he hasn't vomited . . . We're at 300 Muirwood Way, 483-5179."

Stunned, Rosemary put the phone down. Quickly she picked it up again and dialed Kevin's number.

"Kevin? It's Rosemary. I've got a crisis. Grandpa's unconscious and . . ."

She didn't even get to finish the sentence before Kevin hung up. In her upset state, she took it as a rejection. I shouldn't have called him just because I'm upset.

Before Rosemary could finish lashing herself for her mistakes, she heard the front door opening.

"I'm here," Kevin called. "Where are you?"

"In Grandpa's bedroom."

Kevin appeared in the doorway, flushed and breathless. He leaned over Arthur. "Have you called an ambulance?"

"The paramedics are on their way."

"Did they say to do anything while we wait?"

"Not unless he vomits or stops breathing."

"We just have to wait, I guess."

Rosemary started pacing frantically around the room.

"It's my fault, Kev. I've been acting awful lately."

"It's not your fault, Rosemary—it's dumb to think like that. Here's a man who's lost his wife of how many years?"

"Forty-seven."

"Okay, he's lost his wife of forty-seven years. That's what he's hurting from, not something you've done, not some childish tantrum you've thrown."

Leave it to Kevin to tell it straight, Rosemary thought. That's what it's been, all right, a childish tantrum.

"I hear a siren."

Rosemary dashed to the door. Two paramedics were unloading their equipment. With speed and efficiency, they wrote down the facts, checked Arthur's condition, and prepared him for the ambulance ride.

"Is he going to be all right?" Rosemary asked tensely. Her voice was shaky and her hands were clammy.

"He's breathing and that's good," the paramedic replied. "Okay, who's the adult in charge?"

Rosemary pointed to Arthur and shrugged her shoulders.

"My grandma just died, so its him and me." She looked at Kevin, the reality of the situation slowly sinking in. "I'm in charge." There was awe in Rosemary's voice.

Kevin nodded solemnly.

"You want to go with him to the hospital?" one paramedic asked while the other inserted a breathing tube into Arthur's mouth.

"Of course," Rosemary replied.

"Well, you can ride with us if you want, but that'll leave you stranded without transportation at night. Have you a license to drive your grandfather's car?"

"Yes."

"Then why don't you follow the ambulance?"

"Okay."

In a daze, Rosemary watched her grandfather being wheeled out of the house and placed in the ambulance.

"Come on," Kevin prodded. "Hurry up. Lock the house and let's get going."

Rosemary numbly followed instructions, moving like a machine. She pulled out of the garage with a jerk and waited for Kevin to close the door. Then she flipped the car around, and with squealing tires took off in pursuit of the ambulance carrying Arthur.

Never in her wildest dreams had Rosemary ever driven like an ambulance driver. Following in the wake of the flashing red light and the wailing siren, she wove in and out of city traffic at high speed. People stopped for her. Cars stopped for her. Her adrenalin really began to flow. Her face was flushed, her arms strong, her eyes gleaming.

This is great, she thought. With her mind blocking out the reason for the trip, it became one super roller-coaster ride.

"Terrific, huh?" Grinning crazily, Rosemary turned to Kevin. "Like it?"

Kevin's face was ashen. "Rosemary! Slow down," he gasped. "It's illegal."

The ambulance made a sharp right turn into the hospital driveway. Rosemary almost overshot the turn. She braked quickly, spun the wheel, and fought to control the fishtailing reaction.

"Rosemary!" Now Kevin was shouting. "If the police catch you..."

The car careened up the driveway and jolted to a stop beside the ambulance. Mechanically, Rosemary turned off the engine and opened the car door. The minute she stepped out onto the driveway, she began to tremble uncontrollably. Just as her knees buckled under her, a sharp-eyed nurse caught her.

The next thing she knew she was lying down and a nurse was standing over her.

"Grandpa . . ." she mumbled. "Grandpa? Where's Grandpa?"

"It's all right. Take it easy," the nurse said, placing a soothing hand on Rosemary's forehead. "We're taking care of him."

"My grandpa . . ." Rosemary tried to sit up, but dropped back on the pillow, her head spinning. "Where's my grandpa?" She narrowed her eyes to focus more sharply on the nurse's face. Then she whispered, "Is he dead?"

"He's with the doctor. No, he's not dead."

"Is he all right?"

"They pumped his stomach. He'll live, but he'll feel pretty sick in the morning."

"You're sure about that? That he'll live?"

"Yes."

"He's okay? He'll live? You're sure he's okay?" The welcome truth was slowly sinking in. "He'll live . . . he's okay." Rosemary's eyes closed.

"Yes, things are looking good for your grandfather, so now how are you feeling?" the nurse asked. "Aside from your light head, how do you feel?"

"All right, I guess. Why?"

"Well, you came unglued for a while there."

"Just worried about Grandpa," Rosemary mumbled, "that's all."

"His first question was about you, too," the nurse said softly.

"We only have each other. You're sure he's all right?"

"Yes, he's progressing well. By the way, there's a young man waiting to see you."

"Kevin?" Rosemary was trying to fit the missing pieces together in her mind. "How long has he been waiting?"

"Quite a while. Ever since you arrived."

"What time is it?"

"Ten o'clock."

"At night?"

"Definitely night."

Suddenly Kevin was standing in the doorway and the nurse was leaving.

"You can get up any time you feel like it," the nurse said as she moved into the hall, "but do it slowly, okay?"

"Hey, wait," Rosemary called. "Can I see my grandfather?"

"He won't be worth much for a while, but yes, you can see him."

Looking very subdued, Kevin came close to the table where Rosemary lay. She was rubbing her forehead, trying to get her brain back into focus.

"I'm afraid I haven't been very good company for you to-night," she apologized.

"You've had your more sparkling moments," Kevin agreed. He broke into a grin. "But I must say, you provided an out-standing ride behind that ambulance! By tomorrow my pulse rate may be back to normal."

Rosemary held her head. "I think I want to forget that ride." She pulled herself slowly to a sitting position, swung her legs off the table, and waited for her balance to return.

"Does your mother know where you are, Kevin?"

"I phoned and told her. She offered to come down if she could be of any help, but I said she didn't need to."

"I want to see Grandpa," Rosemary said nervously. "Have you seen him?"

"No, they were too busy to bother with me, but they said he was coming out of it all right."

"Let's go and find him." Rosemary slid off the table, grabbed Kevin's hand, and led him into the hall. The nurse spotted them and pointed to Arthur's room.

"He's asleep," she said.

"But is he all right?"

"He seems to be. The doctor wants to talk with you, though."

Rosemary and Kevin stepped into the room and gazed down at the sleeping figure. Arthur looked old and gaunt, but even in sleep he retained his own unique quality of dignity.

"Got a comb?" Rosemary whispered to Kevin.

He found a small one in his jacket pocket and passed it over. Rosemary leaned down and carefully combed the tangles from the wavy white hair. She ran the comb through her own hair before handing it back.

"Let's find the doctor," she whispered.

A woman appeared in the doorway and spoke softly, "I'm Dr. Jacobi. Let's sit down and talk for a moment." She led the way to a conference room.

"Your grandfather will be pale and shaky and will feel very sick in the morning, Rosemary. You understand that, don't you? Don't be too distressed about the way he looks. You probably can take him home tomorrow and let him recover there. But there's more to recovery than that. This man has to go through a mourning period, and you'll have to understand what he's going through."

The doctor fixed her gaze directly on Rosemary. "You'll have to go through your own mourning time, too, so don't be too hard on yourself if you don't like the way you feel sometimes. The main thing for both of you is to have some people in your lives who care—people you can talk to. Now, how about your grandfather? Does he have someone close?"

"Not really. My grandmother was his best friend."

"Then it looks as if you're going to have to move into a new role, Rosemary. And I'd also suggest your trying to get him to join the support group at the Hawthorne Senior Citizen Center. It's been set up to help people adjust to loss." Dr. Jacobi paused. "And you?"

She was studying Rosemary intently. "I see you have a friend."

Kevin beamed.

"You'd better go home and get some sleep now," the doctor advised, "and come back in the morning for your grandfather."

After thanking Dr. Jacobi and the nurses, Rosemary and Kevin walked silently to the lobby. As they passed the snack bar Rosemary paused uncertainly.

"Kevin, I think I'd better get something to eat. I haven't eaten since breakfast."

"No wonder you passed out!"

The counter was closed, but Kevin went to the vending machines and studied the possibilities. "Well, you can get sandwiches and milk here, or we can stop at a coffee shop on the way home. What do you think?"

"I'd better take what I can get right now."

"Okay, two sandwiches? Tuna? Ham? Egg salad?"

"Tuna and ham, I guess."

"And two milks?"

"Sure."

Rosemary reached in her pocket and found only some small change.

"Here, be my guest." Kevin deposited the money in the machine and handed Rosemary her food.

"Thanks, Kev. Want part of it?"

Kevin shook his head. "I ate a candy bar while I was in the waiting room."

"I can eat this in the car if you'll drive."

"Not only will I be glad to drive—I insist!"

Rosemary wasn't sure if he was pretending to be afraid to ride with her, or if she really had scared him half to death.

They left by the front door, walking across the deserted visitors' parking lot to reach the emergency wing of the building. Rosemary recoiled from the memory of her dramatic entrance into the emergency parking lot earlier in the day.

Flashing her a dazzling smile, Kevin opened the door and held the food while she fastened her seat belt.

"You heard what the doctor said, Rosie. You have a friend." He closed the door and went around to the driver's side. "So talk to me," he said softly. "I'm your friend."

Rosemary was drained. Her head ached. She felt ready to cry. She wanted to curl up in a dark corner. It was all she could do to sit up. The last thing she wanted to do was talk. Slowly she folded back the plastic wrap on her sandwiches and ate them in silence.

Kevin didn't press his offer. He kept quiet for a long time. Finally he said, "I didn't mean talk now, you know, Rosemary. I meant later. When you're bothered by something, talk to me. Any time. Don't brood all alone like you always do."

"Yeah," Rosemary murmured, "nobody alone can be as effective as two people working together, right? I know that, Kevin. But talking about feelings has always been hard for me. Maybe it's my Nordic ancestry. Maybe it's my growing up as an only child."

"Maybe you just never tried it."

"Maybe you're right again, Kev."

They retreated into their own thoughts, wrapped in their old comfortable, companionable silence. There was no more talk until they turned onto Muirwood Way.

"Your house is pretty dark and lonely," Kevin said as he stopped in the driveway. "You could sleep at our place."

"Thanks for the offer, but tonight isn't worrying me," Rosemary replied. "I'm so tired I'll be asleep when I hit the pillow. It's tomorrow that's going to be hard. If I can just get Grandpa back here, then I'll be home free."

Kevin opened the garage door and parked the car inside. Going ahead into the house, he turned on lights for Rosemary. After checking that all windows and doors were securely locked, he made one more offer.

"Want me to stay here with you tonight? I can sleep on the couch."

Kevin laughed at the expression on Rosemary's face. "I'll be good, Rosie, I swear."

"No, but thanks," Rosemary replied, feeling touched by his tenderness and protectiveness.

"Okay, would you like me to go to the hospital with you in the morning?"

"I think Grandpa and I had better talk alone tomorrow," Rosemary decided. "But thanks. Thanks for everything, Kev. Good-night."

"Good-night, Rosie."

"Kevin, my name is . . ."

Kevin put a hand softly under Rosemary's chin and studied her eyes for a moment.

"You heard me—good-night, Rosie."

He turned and left quickly, closing the front door softly behind him.

Rosemary stood in the hallway, trying to recall the details of those last few minutes. The searching way Kevin had looked at her sent a tingle down her spine. And the way he had said "You heard me." She knew that was his polite way of saying, "Don't try to make all the rules, Rosemary."

The name Rosie, coming from Kevin, didn't sound the same tonight, she marveled. It sounded kind of nice. I'm surprised. Good-night, Rosie . . . good-night, Rosie. Funny how I used to hate it whenever he used that name. And now it sounds so different.

Rosemary glanced around the house. What a mess I've let this place become, she thought with disgust. After everything

Gram taught me about keeping a place decent, she'd be horrified.

She yawned, feeling her whole body sagging from the letdown. I'll tackle the mess in the morning, she promised and fell into bed.

๑ Chapter 14 ๒

When Rosemary opened her eyes the next morning, her mind was a blur. Bit by bit, she had to piece the picture together. What day is it? Must be Wednesday. Cut school yesterday. To the ridge . . . Grandpa? Grandpa!

Rosemary bolted out of bed and raced through the house, hoping it was just a bad dream, but all the grim reminders were there, softened only by the fact that Arthur had survived. I almost lost Grandpa last night, Rosemary mused, but I've been given another chance.

With the intensity of a contrite sinner doing penance, she tore around, tidying up, vacuuming, putting in a load of laundry, and making out a shopping list. At ten o'clock she phoned the hospital to confirm Arthur's release. While packing some clean clothes in a bag, she remembered she would need her grandfather's hospital insurance card, too. Anything else?

Better take a pillow and a blanket. And a blank check, just in case.

A knock on the door jolted Rosemary from her thoughts. When she opened the door, Kevin was standing on the porch, smiling.

"Didn't you go to school?" Rosemary asked, ignoring the obvious.

"Your grandpa seemed more important to me today. I thought I could do something, like help clean the house maybe?"

Kevin peered beyond Rosemary into the living room. "But you've sure got the place looking good. What's left for me to do?"

Rosemary had an inspiration. "How about going to the market while I'm at the hospital?" She stopped. "That's okay —forget that idea. You don't have a car to carry it all home, and we need a lot of things."

"No, I can do it. My mother doesn't go to work until noon today, so I can use her car. Give me your list."

"I don't know if you can even read my sloppy writing," Rosemary apologized.

"Try me." Kevin took the list and read it out loud, stumbling on a few items and making notes for himself, while Rosemary got some money from Arthur's secret hiding place.

"That's great. It'll help a lot, Kevin. I've got to hurry now and get Grandpa. I hope he's as happy about coming home as I am about getting him back."

Rosemary replayed that thought as she drove to the hospital.

In all of her joy over having her grandfather alive, she hadn't stopped to wonder if he shared her joy. After all—Rosemary shivered at the chilling fact—he did choose to end his life eighteen hours ago. What's different today? The edge was taken off her joy.

At the hospital she went to the office to get the release papers and then to her grandfather's room. Arthur was asleep in his bed.

"Grandpa," Rosemary said softly. The nurse stood back, letting the granddaughter handle the awakening. Rosemary shook the old man's shoulder very gently until his eyelids fluttered and opened slowly.

"Rosemary." Arthur's mouth was like sandpaper, his voice barely audible. "Are you all right, Rosemary?"

"I'm fine, Grandpa." Rosemary paused. "Now that I've got you back."

"I never should have done it," Arthur mumbled. "Never should have . . . selfish . . . just kept thinking of joining Della . . ."

"I know, Grandpa." Tears were streaming down Rosemary's face. "But we can have good times, Gramp. We can. Really."

She reached for the bag of clothes, figuring she had better start some action before they both fell apart.

"Come on, let's get you dressed. It's time to go home."

"But I feel too sick."

"The doctor says that will wear off. Come on," Rosemary urged.

As she talked, she and the nurse eased the limp patient into his clothes and helped him into a wheelchair. Arthur, still dazed and drowsy, passively allowed himself to be wheeled out of the hospital and pulled and pushed into the car, where he promptly fell asleep with his head on the pillow Rosemary had brought along.

When Rosemary pulled into the driveway, Kevin was sitting on the front steps, waiting to greet them. He waved enthusiastically.

"We're home, Grandpa. Wake up! Kevin's here to greet you, too." Rosemary shook Arthur gently until he seemed awake. Kevin opened the car door. "You can walk into the house, can't you?" Rosemary coaxed.

Arthur nodded. With Kevin on one side and Rosemary on the other, he shuffled into the living room and sank onto the couch.

"Welcome home, Mr. Magnuson," Kevin said as he spread a blanket over Arthur and adjusted a pillow under his head.

"Thank you," Arthur sighed. "Thank you, Kevin."

Kevin smiled at the old man and waved a silent good-bye to Rosemary. He backed out of the door, closing it quietly, leaving the Magnusons to begin the reconstruction process.

For a long time Arthur lay with his eyes closed. Rosemary, watching him from the armchair, wondered if her grandfather was sleeping or thinking. Eventually, Arthur stirred and raised a hand as if motioning for Rosemary to come close. She moved over and sat on the floor by the couch.

"I'm very sorry," Arthur murmured, "very sorry I did that to you, Rosemary. I must have been out of my mind."

"It was the depression, Grandpa. We both were pretty down."

"I was only thinking . . . of Della." Arthur's words, barely audible, came slowly. "Only when I was . . . almost gone . . . did I realize I was . . . leaving you behind, Rosemary. And then it was . . . too late."

"Almost too late," Rosemary corrected. "Not too late." She patted her grandfather's trembling hand. "You're back, Grandpa."

"You didn't tell Sigrid, did you?" There was new anxiety in Arthur's voice.

"No, I was too busy to even think about that."

". . . don't want her to know, ever."

"Okay, Grandpa. It's just between us. And Kevin."

"Thank you."

The old man nodded slowly, his eyelids drooping. Rosemary rushed to keep him awake. "Hey, did you see how good the place looks? All neat and clean? And we have food. Kevin went and bought that for us. And I'm going to cook us Gram's recipe for vegetable soup tonight."

"I'm impressed," Arthur said with a trace of a smile. "May I sleep till dinnertime?"

"Sure, Gramp. I'll take care of things."

"I can see that you already have," Arthur replied.

"Yeah," Rosemary agreed giving her grandfather a friendly little poke in the arm. "At the moment, I'm the adult in charge." She grinned, and Arthur fell into a deep sleep.

All day long Rosemary was a hovering nurse, watching for changes in her patient—his breathing, his facial expression, his shifting positions. Twice, when Arthur padded into the bathroom in his stocking feet, Rosemary thought her grandfather was ready to wake up and look alive. But both times Arthur was almost trancelike, not seeming to be aware of the passage of time or of Rosemary's presence.

Finally, when Rosemary had two dinner trays ready, she took a wet washcloth to Arthur and insisted that he wake up and wash his face for dinner. Arthur obediently sat up, washed his face, blinked a few times, and began to look more alert.

"That was very nice," he told Rosemary as he sipped the last spoonful of soup. "You're a good cook, just like your grandmother."

Even more than the praise, Rosemary liked the fact that her grandfather was starting to act like himself again.

"What day is it, Rosemary?"

"Wednesday."

"You've missed a whole day of school."

Rosemary didn't plan to tell her grandfather it had been two days and probably was going to be more. She brushed off Arthur's concern. "No problem."

Rosemary took the trays to the kitchen and cleared away the sink mess. Next she moved Arthur into the armchair and turned on the TV. Together they watched some of their usual shows, passing a comfortable evening. At nine o'clock, when Arthur decided he was ready to go to bed, Rosemary helped

135

him into the bedroom, laid out his clean pajamas, and turned back the blankets for him.

"Feeling better, Grandpa?" she asked as Arthur settled down into the bed.

"Yes, much better. I don't see how I could ever feel worse than I did. Thank you for being so helpful, Rosemary."

With her grandfather in bed, Rosemary went into the living room and phoned Kevin.

"I'm going to stick around tomorrow," she told him, "just in case he needs anything . . . Uh huh, he seems to be feeling better . . . Yeah, he ate a good dinner . . . Thanks to your shopping, there's finally some decent food in the house . . . Grandpa's right, you know, Kevin—true blue, through and through."

Rosemary waited through a long silence at Kevin's end of the line. "No, Kev, I really mean it. . . . Thanks, I'll miss you, too. . . . Tell the Lees hi for me. Good-night."

Rosemary straightened up the living room and went to bed. Lying in the darkness, she mulled over the happenings of the past two days. Only forty-eight hours, she thought—in only forty-eight hours I've got Grandpa back and things are okay with Kevin. How is it possible for so much to change in a few hours? Three people, and not one of us is the same. Grandpa's not the same, I'm not the same, even Kevin's not the same.

Rosemary's thoughts lingered on her special friend with the unruly hair and the tender brown eyes, who seemed to know what she was feeling before she did. How come he's so different all of a sudden? she wondered.

⇘ Chapter 15 ⇗

"Well, that's more like it," Rose-
mary told Benjamin Bear the next morning as she opened her
eyes. "I have a grandfather across the hall instead of an empty
room." She straightened Benjamin's tie and looked around for
an interesting place for him to spend the day. She settled on
the desk by the window, where there was some early morning
warmth.

The sun, streaming through the sheer curtains, was full of
promises. Rosemary stepped out of bed into a puddle of sunshine and stretched like a cat, letting the relaxation move from
one place to another until she had eased the knots that had
tied up her muscles since the moment she had discovered
Arthur on the bed. She showered, dressed, and went to the
kitchen to fix some breakfast for herself and Arthur. Rosemary
was hoping for large miracles.

What she got was a small miracle. Arthur, alert instead of drowsy, had got himself out of bed and moved to the couch, but that was the full extent of his activity. He passively accepted the breakfast tray Rosemary brought him and steadfastly rejected all of her suggestions.

"Why don't you shave, Grandpa? You'll feel a lot better without that scratchy stubble on your face."

Arthur brushed off the idea.

"Here's your morning paper, Grandpa. You can catch up with what's happening in the world."

Arthur resisted. "I don't really care."

"It's a beautiful day. Why don't you take your coffee out into the garden and relax with it in the lawn chair?"

"Maybe later."

Rosemary kept trying, but her role of nurse seemed to be changing rapidly into something else, something more like companion-housekeeper. She hovered over her grandfather, making conversation, entertaining him, picking up things he dropped, trying to keep up his morale. It was her job, she felt, to keep her grandfather from slipping back into deep depression. And that burden grew heavier and heavier for Rosemary to carry. What if—she kept thinking, what if I can't? She wasn't home free, after all.

Arthur began to sense the tension in his granddaughter. "Why are you always looking at me like that?" he asked.

"Like what?" Rosemary played dumb.

"Like you're expecting me to do it again if you leave me alone."

Rosemary was taken off guard by the honesty of her grandfather's remark. "Yeah, I'm a little scared, I guess."

Arthur's expression was pained. "I promise you, Rosemary, I will never again try to take death out of God's hands. But even with that promise, I know your fear will remain." Arthur's anguish surfaced in a deep sigh. "Making my granddaughter carry the scars of my bad judgment is heavy punishment for me."

"I'm all right, Grandpa." Rosemary had a lump in her throat that made it hard to reassure her grandfather.

"But," Arthur continued, "you mustn't keep expecting me to act lighthearted and cheerful. I don't feel lighthearted and cheerful. Just allow me my pain in losing Della."

Confronting the facts did ease Rosemary's anxiety somewhat. She no longer felt compelled to track her grandfather wherever he went. But she did wish she could ease his loneliness. What's he going to do with his days while I'm at school, she wondered, if he can't even see a good reason for getting up in the morning?

By afternoon the job of spirit raiser had begun to wear thin with Rosemary. She had geared up rapidly to meet the medical crisis, and she had handled that well. But that part was finished, and the newer problem had no end in sight. The prospect of trying to make an unhappy person happy overwhelmed Rosemary. Her own spirits sank so rapidly that by four o'clock the two Magnusons were equally depressed.

"I'm going to see if Kevin's home," Rosemary said. Whether he was or wasn't, she had to get out of the house into some other world. She left Arthur sitting in the armchair, alone with his thoughts.

Kevin was just coming down Muirwood Way as Rosemary approached his house. "Hi," he called. "I'm late because some new kids from Colorado enrolled in school today. Were you waiting long?"

"Just got here," Rosemary replied.

"Want to come in? Need a sandwich or anything?" Kevin offered.

"No, I've been around the kitchen all day, remember?"

"How's your grandfather feeling?"

"Probably better than I am!"

"Oh?" Kevin looked startled. "Another casualty?" He dropped down on the front steps and motioned for Rosemary to sit down, too. "What's the matter?"

"I'm stuck with an impossible job!" Suddenly exploding, Rosemary poured out the frustrations of the day. "I spent a whole stupid day doing things to try and make him contented. Get his newspaper. Bring him things. Sit by him. Be friendly." She paused in disgust. "Arf, arf. Look closely. Have I grown furry ears and a tail yet? I've been nothing all day but a friendly dog, wagging my tail to make him smile, waiting to have my head patted."

Rosemary stopped, a little ashamed of her feelings. "I love him," she apologized. "I want him happy."

"But you don't want to be a cute and cuddly puppy following him around forever, right?"

Kevin had hit it straight on. Rosemary was relieved he could put it in words for her. For a day or a week or even a month, she could handle the role, but the long-range prospects were overwhelming.

"What he needs . . ." Rosemary's frustrations were still surfacing. "What he needs is . . ."

"A friendly dog!" Kevin said. They stared at one another, stunned by their synchronized thinking.

"That's right." Rosemary was rolling the idea around in her mind with some amazement. "That's absolutely right. A friendly dog could beat me easily at most of the things I did today. Right now Grandpa needs a twenty-four-hour-a-day companion who doesn't care if he shaves, who likes him inactive, and who won't feel guilty if he's depressed."

"Do you think he would get himself a dog?" Kevin asked. "If he would, you'd be freed to do the special things that only Rosemary Magnuson can do for her grandfather. Wouldn't that be great?"

"Terrific! I know Grandpa's always liked dogs, but Gram was allergic to fur." For a moment Rosemary was carried away with enthusiasm. "Terrif . . ." Her excitement faded like a balloon deflating. "No, Grandpa won't go out and buy a dog," she groaned. "He won't even go out into the garden. Right now he's not going to make some big decision like adopting an animal."

"And the trouble is, right now is when he needs it most," Kevin mused. "Maybe you could soften him up to the idea."

"If I brought up the subject and he said no, the issue would be dead forever. That's too risky."

"Do you think we could get a dog for him, and if he didn't want to keep it, we could take it back?" Kevin was working all the angles.

"I don't think they sell pets on approval," Rosemary said. "You can't try them on for size and take them back if they don't fit."

"I'll bet if your grandpa and the right dog got together, nothing would ever get them apart, Rosemary. I'll just bet. He's that kind of man."

"I'll kind of hint around and see how he reacts to the idea," Rosemary replied. "It sure sounds like what he needs, but I'm afraid I already know the answer."

"Well, try anyway." Kevin's mind suddenly flipped to a different subject. "Oh, by the way, I saw Jackson and Shirley, and they asked about you."

"What did you say?"

"I told them your grandfather wasn't feeling well and you were staying with him." Kevin paused a moment. "Rosemary, I had no idea you had taught them so much English. They're doing great."

"I didn't do it, Kevin. They were just afraid to speak. They studied English in Hong Kong, but they were afraid that in America no one would be able to understand them, so they pretended they didn't know any English at all. They've been gaining confidence, and now they're racing ahead."

"Yeah, confidence is what the newcomers need. Anyhow, they said to tell you they like their work at the print and copy center."

"That's good." Rosemary's attention was distracted by a growing uneasiness about being away from Arthur so long. "I'd better get back to Grandpa now."

She kneeled in a begging position in front of Kevin, her tongue out, panting like a dog. "Arf, arf."

Kevin laughed and gave her a friendly shove toward home. She returned to the house with her mind churning, struggling to come up with a foolproof scheme to get her grandfather to consider buying himself a dog.

Rosemary's initial approach was casual. "Kevin said hi to you, Grandpa."

"That's always nice."

She got busy starting dinner, suspecting that a bored Arthur would join her in the kitchen. When he did, she eased into the subject by way of a sociable question that would take them both back to happier times.

"Grandpa, when I was growing up, why didn't we ever have a dog? Whenever I mentioned it as a kid, you always told me I shouldn't bring the subject up to Gram." Rosemary held her breath for fear her scheme was too apparent. If Arthur smelled a conspiracy, he would balk.

"Well, Della was always allergic to animal fur, and . . ." Arthur had started reminiscing.

Interrupting his reverie, Rosemary put the conversation back on track. "Did you know that I was always wishing we could have a dog, Grandpa? Ever since I was little?"

"Yes, Rosemary. Your grandmother and I often talked about that. Della felt badly that you were deprived of a pet because of her health. She used to say 'Children and puppies belong together, and an only child needs one especially.' It was one of her real disappointments that she could never get you a dog." Arthur paused, lost in thought. "I kind of missed it, too, while you were growing up."

Better not push any further, Rosemary decided. I've laid the groundwork. Now I'd better stop.

Arthur, apparently, had gone as far as he wished with his memories and changed the subject.

"I really think you should get back to school tomorrow, Rosemary. You've already missed too much."

The idea of getting out sounded good to Rosemary, but she hesitated. "Will you be okay?"

"Of course." Arthur looked over at his granddaughter with a trace of the old twinkle in his eye. "Are you asking if I'll be good while the adult in charge is away?"

"You got it, Gramp." Rosemary grinned, seeing that Arthur was making a little progress already.

❧ Chapter 16 ❧

Rosemary surprised herself by waking a half hour before the alarm went off the next morning. She lay in bed, letting her mind gradually come into focus.

It's Friday . . . have to get back to school. Seems like I've been a thousand miles and a hundred days away from it. Kind of good to be getting back. Strange, though . . . no one will ever know how much has happened in just two days. No one but Kevin knows the scene I came home to on Tuesday, or what happened to me that night, or what Grandpa is really going through. And no one but Kevin knows that I'm a lot more interested in getting a dog for Grandpa than I am in today's classwork. People really don't know a whole lot.

She reached over and turned off the alarm, smiling at one final observation. And no one knows how different Kevin is from what I thought he was. He's really kind of—special, I guess.

Rosemary straightened Benjamin's back and propped him against the wall with a pat. Slinging her legs off the bed, she sat up. So today the new Rosemary Magnuson faces the old school crowd. Oh well, we never did know that much about each other, she concluded.

Arthur wandered into the kitchen while Rosemary was eating her breakfast.

"Hungry?" she asked, offering to fix him something.

"No, thanks. Just came to visit. The day will be pretty long."

Rosemary wondered if she should say that a dog could brighten the long days, but she decided not to chance it. Arthur might begin to suspect she was scheming.

"This is the morning you're treating yourself to a shave, I guess." Rosemary hoped she was planting a positive notion. To her, the stubble that was almost a beard was a symbol of Arthur's lack of concern for himself. "It'll be a treat to come home to a clean-shaven face." She looked to Arthur for confirmation. "Right?"

Arthur shook his head. "Not a chance."

Rosemary wasn't sure whether to believe the denial or not. At least she had tried. Her grandfather was up, anyway, and he wasn't sitting in that armchair looking glassy eyed, which was promising.

Arthur waved good-bye wistfully as Rosemary took her books and walked down Muirwood Way.

Kevin was waiting on his steps, anxious for news. "Any progress with your grandfather on the dog idea?"

"I'm not sure, Kev. He said we never had a dog when I was

a kid because of Gram's allergies. And he also admitted he'd kind of missed having one."

"Sounds hopeful."

"Well, I don't think it means he'll up and decide to get himself one right now."

"Keep your campaign going over the weekend," Kevin suggested, "and if he seems receptive, maybe we could go to the SPCA next week and just see who's up for adoption. We might con him into it with some sad story about this lonely little puppy with the soulful eyes who's waiting to be loved."

"Kevin!" Rosemary stared at him in amazement. "I had no idea you were a schemer." She shook her head and chuckled. "And here I always thought you were Old-tell-it-straight-Kev. Instead I discover that you're positively conniving."

"Yeah," he agreed proudly. "It works wonders for a good cause."

When they reached the entrance to the school, Kevin was swept away by some Newcomers Service Club business. Rosemary scanned the crowd for Shirley or Jackson. She still hadn't found them when the bell rang, so she gave up and went to first period.

Classes didn't seem very important to Rosemary while she had so many other pressing things on her mind. She figured she could hit the textbooks later. First she had to get Grandpa stabilized somehow.

When lunchtime came, Rosemary started looking for the Lees in the locker area. The crowd thinned out rapidly, and she could see she had missed them, so she headed for the cafeteria. Just as she was going in, Shirley and Jackson approached the door from the other direction. Their first words of greeting reflected their concern for the elderly.

"How is the grandfather?" Jackson inquired. "Kevin said he was ill."

"He's better," Rosemary replied, "but it's going to take some time. He's very depressed."

Shirley looked uncertain. "Depressed?"

"Sad," Rosemary explained.

Shirley understood. "Yes, you are sad, too, aren't you?"

Rosemary nodded.

As they went through the food service line together, Jackson said, "We have missed you at lunch, Rosemary."

"I've missed being here. Have they had any foods you didn't know?"

"Yes, sometimes we had to point," Jackson admitted.

"But we are very improved," Shirley added proudly.

With their trays loaded, Rosemary looked around the cafeteria for Kevin. When she spotted him in a crowd, eating with the young men from Colorado, she led the way to an empty table and settled down to enjoy her time with Shirley and Jackson.

"Tell me about your jobs," she said as she started her lunch.

"It is going well," Jackson replied. "Uncle does much business."

"Our work is fine quality," Shirley added.

Rosemary was touched by her sincerity.

"I'm sure it is."

"You must come and see the shop, Rosemary," Shirley suggested.

"I'd like to. I sort of grew up in a printing shop."

"Grew up in a printing shop?" Jackson was stunned. "You had no home? You lived in a printing shop?"

"That's a figure of speech," Rosemary explained. "Grandpa owned his own printing business for thirty years, and I used to play around the shop when my grandmother went there to help him."

"His own shop for thirty years!" Jackson marveled.

"Yes, Grandpa came to America when he was just your age, Jackson. He started out as a delivery boy for a printer and ended up owning the business."

"Really?" Jackson was captivated by this real evidence of the American dream. "He has seen many changes then, hasn't he?"

"Uh huh, I've heard him talk about the days when, on some jobs, every letter had to be set by hand."

"We use wonderful new machines at our shop. I enjoy them." Jackson's pride was apparent. "I want to learn the business."

"And some day own the company!" Rosemary added for him.

They both laughed, knowing that there was a lot of truth in the joke.

"By the way, do they ever need another worker?" Rosemary asked, suddenly hit by a new idea. "Maybe a relief person to fill in when someone's out or when business is extra heavy? I couldn't be gone all the time while Grandpa is so lonely, but I surely could use some occasional money. And I'd like that kind of work, I know."

"I'll ask Ben," Jackson promised.

"He might want someone for Wednesdays when Kee goes to night school," Shirley suggested.

"That would be wonderful," Rosemary replied. "Tell Ben you know a terrific young woman who's dependable and follows orders and learns fast. And," Rosemary added with a teasing twinkle in her eye, "is a perfect human being."

"And anything else?" Jackson asked, trying to keep a straight face.

The lunch period passed too quickly. Rosemary was enjoying the conversation and hated to stop in order to go to afternoon classes.

She endured sixth period, her mind preoccupied with thoughts of a possible job. When seventh period came, her thoughts shifted to the situation at home. Teaming a lonely old man up with a happy little dog would relieve so many problems. If I can swing that, she figured, then I could get a job with a clear conscience.

When school was out, Rosemary hurried to the courtyard and hung around, hoping Kevin would come. He hadn't shown up by three-fifteen, so she walked home alone.

As Rosemary turned onto Muirwood Way, her spirits rose. Arthur's car was parked in front of the garage instead of inside, where she had left it. Great, she thought, Grandpa's been out somewhere. I was afraid he was thinking of himself as an invalid who wouldn't ever be going outside again.

"I'm home, Grandpa," Rosemary called as she unlocked the door.

"Hello, Rosemary." Arthur was sitting in the armchair, clean shaven and well dressed.

"Hey, who's the classy dude in my living room? What became of the guy with the stubbly beard and rumpled clothes?"

Arthur rubbed his chin and tried to look casual. "It itched," he confessed.

"And I see you've been running around town, too."

"Well, I needed some shaving cream. And I wanted to do a couple of errands."

"Great. I'm proud of you, Gramp."

"Save the congratulations, Rosemary. After I'd gone a ways I discovered I'm not yet back to full vigor. In fact, I shouldn't have been behind a wheel at all. I was a menace." Arthur paused, his eyes meeting his granddaughter's. "Could I impose on you to be my driver for a few errands in the morning?"

Rosemary saw her own plans for Saturday morning dissolving, but if Arthur wanted to do anything at all, she would certainly encourage the activity. "No problem," she agreed. "No problem at all."

As the evening wore on, Rosemary was amazed at her grandfather's high spirits. She didn't dare hope they would last, but any good moments were very welcome.

And while he's so mellow, she figured, why not put in a

pitch for my project. "Grandpa, wouldn't you like to have the company of a dog during your long days? A happy little guy with a wagging tail?" Rosemary held her breath and waited for the answer.

"No, Rosemary. I don't think I want the emotional strain of adding a new family member right now. I just don't feel up to it."

"Just think about it," she urged. "Okay?"

"I'll think."

Well, I didn't win, Rosemary thought, but I didn't lose, either. I'll keep softening him up to the idea during the weekend, and maybe Kevin can work his charms on him, too. He has his own brand of persuasion, and it's very effective.

If we convince Grandpa, Rosemary gloated, it'll be so great. If only we can convince him!

❧ Chapter 17 ❧

Early on Saturday morning Rosemary heard Arthur stirring. The sun hadn't reached her bed, the birds weren't chirping, the paper hadn't hit the porch. I don't believe it, she thought; I wanted to sleep in. She pulled her pillow over her face, determined not to start Saturday prematurely. Actually, the plan for the day ahead wasn't so terrific that she wanted to start it at all. Driving someone around for errands was hardly the perfect Saturday morning.

Through the pillow Rosemary could tell that her grandfather was quietly closing the bedroom door so he wouldn't disturb her, but the damage was already done. Rosemary was awake, and she wasn't glad. Giving up on the sleeping, she threw the pillow across the room in disgust. How can I sleep when I know he wants to get going early! Why was I born with a stupid conscience? Why couldn't I just make him wait?

Grumbling all the way, Rosemary dressed and staggered into the kitchen. "What are we playing today?" she asked grouchily. "The early bird catches the worm? Or is it rise and shine?"

"I closed your door so you could sleep." Arthur wasn't at all apologetic, and this hit Rosemary wrong. She nursed her grudge silently while she ate, feeling a little proud that she wasn't saying all the unpleasant things she was thinking.

Arthur seemed strangely serene. He fixed his coffee, eggs, and toast in a rather energetic fashion that was quite different from his recent morose manner. He didn't react to any of the irritating actions that were designed to show Rosemary's annoyance. Seemingly oblivious to her displeasure, Arthur calmly ate his breakfast and savored his coffee.

"I'd like to leave at nine," he said, "if that's convenient."

Rosemary wanted to make some barbed comment, but she restrained herself. Gram had always been horrified when Rosemary was rude to her grandfather, so Rosemary had learned to carry on private skirmishes in her mind.

"Is nine convenient?" Arthur asked, having received no signal from his granddaughter.

"Yeah, Grandpa, that's okay." Rosemary's words were grudging.

Promptly at nine, Arthur put on a jacket and stood around, clearly anxious to get started. Rosemary was moving slowly, baffled by her grandfather's urgency. Finally she picked up her keys, put on a jacket, and said, "Let's go." She backed the car out of the garage and waited for Arthur to get in.

"Where to, Grandpa?"

"Crocker Street and Sixteenth."

Rosemary didn't even bother to ask what was down there. She simply drove in silence. They went quite a way beyond the main business district into an area that was unfamiliar to Rosemary.

"Now just stay on this one all the way," Arthur instructed as she turned onto Sixteenth Street.

When they came to Crocker Street, Rosemary looked doubtfully at the warehouses on both corners. "Are you sure you have the right address, Grandpa?"

"Yes," Arthur seemed confident. "There's a parking lot you can use halfway down the block."

"But that's the Humane Society," Rosemary pointed out.

"I know. Della left a small contribution for them in her will."

"Oh." Rosemary found Della's bequest touching. "It's just like Gram to do that, isn't it!" With a changed attitude, she parked the car and waited for Arthur to get out. "I'll stay here while you handle it," she told her grandfather."

"I'd like you to come in, Rosemary. There's a young lady I want you to meet."

"Come on, Grandpa. You know how I am with strangers."

"Gretchen is nice," Arthur persisted. "Della would want you to meet her."

Rosemary wouldn't argue with that. She didn't want to mar Della's gift with any unpleasantness, so she got out of the car and meekly followed her grandfather into the building.

"Hello, Mr. Magnuson," the receptionist said. "You came back to see Gretchen?"

"Yes," Arthur replied. "Could we be alone with her?"

"Of course. I'll have her meet you in the visitor's patio. You know where it is."

"Yes, thank you." Arthur motioned for Rosemary to follow him.

This is more ceremony than is necessary to deliver Gram's gift, she thought as they entered an enclosed brick patio and sat down in two garden chairs.

Just then the sliding door opened and a young woman greeted them.

"Gretchen got the full beauty treatment from our grooming department yesterday after you saw her and liked her, Mr. Magnuson. Come on, sweetheart. Mr. Magnuson is here to see you again." The young woman was urging a shy dog to step into the patio. "Isn't she gorgeous now? I'll leave you three alone."

The woman backed through the door and closed it, leaving a slim, blonde, dark-eyed little dog to size up her visitors.

"Grandpa, what on earth are you up to?" Rosemary was dumbfounded.

"This is Gretchen, Rosemary. Do you like her?"

"Of course. Who wouldn't? She's adorable!"

Gretchen was already nuzzling Arthur's hands.

"I feel certain that Della would have wanted me to get you a dog, Rosemary, first thing. Don't you think she would have?"

Rosemary could hardly grasp the situation. While she and Kevin had been conspiring to get Arthur interested in a dog, he had already picked one out, presumably for Rosemary!

"Of course," Arthur added hastily, "you can go in and look at all the others. There might be another one you'd prefer."

Rosemary looked at Gretchen and Arthur, gazing adoringly into each other's eyes. They belong together, she thought. They're crazy about each other already.

"No, Grandpa. Gretchen's just right."

"Here, Rosemary, get acquainted with her." Arthur turned the dog so they could greet each other. Gretchen acknowledged Rosemary and returned immediately to Arthur.

"Do you like her?" Arthur asked eagerly.

"Sure. She's great." Rosemary turned serious. "The only problem is that I'm not home that much, so most of the training would fall to you, Grandpa. You're the one who'd be with her all day long." Now Rosemary was playing the game to the hilt. "I don't feel right imposing on you, Grandpa, having you take on the work of training and caring for a dog, just so I can have the luxury of enjoying a pet in the evenings without any of the work."

"Oh, I wouldn't really mind, Rosemary." Arthur was trying not to sound too eager. "I could deal with it. Remember I raised a second generation after my first round, so why not go for round three?" Arthur took the little blonde face in his big hands. "Don't you agree, Gretchen?"

"It sounds great to me," Rosemary said, "if you're sure you won't be bothered by all the babysitting."

"She won't be too much trouble," Arthur said confidently. "Will you, Gretchen?" The dog's tail thumped furiously.

"Well, then let's go ahead and adopt her," Rosemary urged.

Arthur was like a child who had just selected his own Christmas gift. "Perfect choice, don't you think?"

"Perfect," Rosemary agreed, stroking Gretchen's ears.

When the paperwork was completed, they stopped in the Humane Society's small pet store to get some food and vitamins. While Rosemary shopped for the things that the instruction sheet said Gretchen would need, Arthur was selecting a handful of toys.

"Do you think this one is too big for her mouth?" he asked Rosemary.

"Well, her mouth will grow," Rosemary suggested.

"No, I want her to have fun now. We'll get the little size instead. Do you want a bed for her, Rosemary?"

"I think she'd be happy in a box with a blanket," Rosemary replied.

"No, let's get this bed for her. It's nice. The pillow is stuffed with cedar shavings."

While Arthur paid for the purchases, Gretchen was nosing curiously around the shop, trailing the scents of other dogs that had passed through the store.

"Come on, little girl," Arthur called. "We're going home." He picked up the leash and started out the door. "Oh, here, do you want to lead your dog to the car, Rosemary?"

"I'll carry the supplies, Grandpa. You can be trusted to get her safely into the car, I'm sure."

Rosemary chuckled to herself as she drove home. Arthur was too busy with Gretchen to notice the knowing little smile on his granddaughter's face. Wait till I tell Kevin, she kept thinking. Just wait till I tell him we've been outschemed by a master.

She let Arthur and Gretchen communicate with one another for a while, but eventually her curiosity got the best of her.

"Grandpa, were you really that weak and shaky behind the wheel yesterday?"

"Yes, Rosemary, I really was. But today I seem to be getting some spring back into my step."

Rosemary glanced over at Arthur, who already was acting like the classic caricature of the doting grandparent. "Are you sure you won't mind babysitting?" she asked jokingly.

"No," he replied in all seriousness, "I'm glad to do it to help you."

"Thanks, Grandpa." Rosemary was serious, too.

As they neared home, Rosemary suddenly remembered the original plan. "What about your other errands, Grandpa?"

"This is the only one I had in mind. But I had to have you along to decide on your dog."

"Sneaky, aren't you!"

Arthur smiled with obvious pride and stroked Gretchen. "I think you made a wise decision, Rosemary."

"Frankly, Grandpa, I think Gretchen made the decision. And you're right, it was a very wise one. She knows a soft touch when she sees one, and, believe me, that little lady's already got you all figured out."

"It's funny—I was always an easy mark for anything Della

ever wanted. Rosemary, do you suppose this young lady senses the same soft spot in me that Della did?"

"Either that, or else you see in Gretchen some of the same things that you liked in Gram."

"Hmmn," Arthur replied, studying Gretchen closely.

As soon as they reached home, Rosemary carried in the dog bed and supplies while Arthur led Gretchen into the house.

"Now I'm going to run down and get Kevin," Rosemary called.

Arthur, engrossed in giving Gretchen a guided tour of the premises, called back, "Good idea."

Rosemary chuckled all the way to Kevin's and waited impatiently at the door to share the news with him.

"You'll never believe it," she blurted out while Kevin was still opening the door. "We've been outschemed, outplotted, and outmaneuvered by a pro. Listen to this one. Grandpa wanted me to drive him around, you know . . ."

Kevin pulled Rosemary through the door and eased her onto the couch, never even breaking the flow of her tale. She piled detail upon detail until she finally stumbled upon an observation that summed it all up. "I think I've figured out what Gretchen's appeal is, Kevin. She's shy, but wants to be friendly, and she's cute, but she doesn't try to show off."

Rosemary looked at Kevin. For a moment he was lost in thought. At last he nodded slowly.

"That's a winning combination in anyone." He looked at Rosemary with an expression she had never seen in him. "Do you think it's possible that your grandpa found in Gretchen the same kind of qualities that he sees in you?"

Rosemary's mouth dropped open and she stared at Kevin. For a moment she looked away in embarrassment, then turned back to study his face.

"You're serious," she concluded.

"Trust me," he replied softly, motioning at the same time for Rosemary to join him. "Come on, let's go see this new Magnuson girl. Maybe I'll like her better than the original," he teased.

Rosemary gave Kevin a gentle punch and began to grin as they walked down the block, recalling all their plotting to ensnare Arthur, only to be outdone by Arthur himself.

❧ Chapter 18 ❧

Rosemary opened her eyes the next morning and discovered she felt different. As she searched tentatively in her mind for reasons, she straightened Benjamin Bear's bow and rubbed his back.

"How long have we been without Gram now?" she asked him. "It's one, two, three, four weeks next Tuesday. That's a month, Benj."

Flinging out her arms exultantly, Rosemary cheered herself on. We got through a month. Looking good! She stretched her legs, her toes, and felt warmed by the glow of success.

She swung her legs off the bed and stood up, pleased to find that her knees were no longer made of rubber. The total exhaustion that had plagued her since Della's death was gone.

Basking in the sunlight that streamed through her east window, Rosemary thought fondly of the little blonde dog who had managed these miracles. Her dog. Hers. She must not forget.

For a moment, Rosemary choked up. That's the way Grandpa is. If the dog had been for himself, he'd have said "Forget it." He'd have gone ahead and dealt with his loneliness all alone. But when he thought I needed a dog to ease my loneliness, his answer was "Let's do it now." What a sweet guy!

Lost in a sentimental reverie, Rosemary dressed, made her bed, and headed for the kitchen to fix some breakfast. And to greet Gretchen, who had been such a good little dog. Quiet all night long, alone in a strange place.

Rosemary opened the door slowly so as not to bump the nose she was sure would be pressed against it.

"Good morning, Gretchen." She was whispering so she wouldn't awaken Arthur.

"Gretchen? Hey, Gretchen!"

There was no dog in the kitchen. Hmm, what's going on? Maybe I'm whispering for nothing, Rosemary thought. Maybe Grandpa got up early and took Gretchen for a walk. No, that's not it—you don't take the dog's bed with you on a walk.

Better check Grandpa's room, Rosemary figured. She tip-toed down the hall and peeked into the bedroom. Arthur was sleeping peacefully, and Gretchen was curled up in his arms. The dog opened her eyes, sensing Rosemary's presence, but didn't stir. As a greeting to Rosemary she flapped her tail softly. Arthur shifted his position and opened his eyes. When he saw Rosemary in the doorway, he hastily pulled the comforter over Gretchen, trying to hide her.

"Good morning, Rosemary."

"Hi, Grandpa. Hi, Gretchen."

"She was lonely," Arthur explained guiltily. "I brought her bed in here, so her whining and yelping wouldn't wake you up."

"Right."

"And when she got cold, I let her get under the blanket. The first night in a new home is a hard adjustment for a puppy."

"Right, Grandpa. And besides, the kid's cute and cuddly and a wonderful con artist."

"Yeah," Arthur agreed lamely. "So much for my theories of child discipline. Let's face it, I'm a soft touch."

"Why not!" Rosemary said with a grin.

It was clear that Arthur and Gretchen were going to take good care of each other, so Rosemary hastily threw together a plan. She could grab this opportunity to be alone for a while on the ridge trail. It was time to do some thinking, and that was the place to do it.

"You guys go ahead and doze," she told Arthur. "After breakfast I'm going to run over to the ridge, so don't be worried if I'm gone for a while. Will you be okay?"

"Hmm. Will we be all right?" Arthur asked Gretchen as she nuzzled his chin. "I believe we will, Rosemary. Enjoy the fresh air and sunshine. There should be lots of joggers and hikers enjoying the trail this morning. It will be nice up there." Arthur's tone was lighthearted and warm.

This was like old times for Rosemary, except that now a day of freedom from worry about her grandfather seemed like total luxury, a blessing for which she was thankful.

Rosemary quickly ate breakfast, packed a lunch, and took off before anything could ruin her plan. She went straight to her favorite hillside, a few yards off the trail, and sprawled out facing the sea. For a while she just soaked up the setting, her mind floating free. Gradually she began to focus more closely on her changed status in life. And finally, she plunged into her first clearheaded decision making since the death of Della. By afternoon she had simplified her list of priorities. She counted them off on her fingers one last time before leaving for home.

I have to catch up on my schoolwork.

I have to work out a new division of household labor to cover the things Gram always did.

I want to work with Shirley and Jackson at the copy center a couple of nights a week, if their uncle will hire me.

I want to take better care of my friendship with Kevin. He's a lot nicer to me than I am to him, and he deserves better.

"That's it," Rosemary murmured, "two have-to's and two want-to's." It was a relief to have everything finally clear. The basic essentials—school, Grandpa, work, and Kevin. I'll be okay if I can keep those four areas in order, she said to the wind.

When Rosemary returned home, she found her grandfather sitting in a garden chair in the backyard, serenely watching a friendly game of tag between Della's birds, who felt they owned the birdbath, and Gretchen, who thought she owned the whole yard. Arthur looked so relaxed and comfortable that Rosemary sat down in the other lawn chair and began telling him about the priorities she had established during her day.

Arthur listened without interrupting. He started to react when Rosemary was through.

"I agree with Number One, Rosemary. School has to be the highest priority. And this ties in with Number Two—you can't have enough time for schoolwork if you're trying to run a household. So I'm going to help out by taking on the major housekeeping chores. You keep your room clean, do your own laundry, and fix your breakfast, and I'll try to do the rest."

"But that's not a fair division," Rosemary protested. "At least count on me for washing the dinner dishes and cooking a weekend dinner. How's that?"

"Sounds good," Arthur agreed. "Now, about Number Three —getting a job. I don't approve of that, Rosemary. I'm sorry if this disappoints you. But jobs and schoolwork don't mix well. You need time for your homework."

It seemed premature to march into battle on a job that hadn't been offered to her, so Rosemary passed the whole issue off lightly. "No one's offered me a job, Grandpa, so don't lie awake worrying about that one."

"All right." Arthur was moving on to a less controversial priority. "Number Four—taking better care of your friendship with Kevin. May I say that's an intelligent decision, Rosemary. He's quite special."

Rosemary poked Arthur's arm in a friendly way. They understood each other perfectly on her fourth priority.

With the challenges clarified, Rosemary embarked the next day on a vigorous program of reordering her life. Her badly neglected schoolwork came first. The teachers, having been told by the counselor of the death of Rosemary's grandmother and the resultant adjustments at home, gave her the month's makeup work so she could catch up with the other students. The load was astounding when the makeup work was added to the current work.

And so priorities One and Two began to dominate the Magnuson household. A daily pattern emerged in which Rosemary paid attention in class and lugged home piles of homework. An unexpected and unacknowledged casualty of this concentration was priority Number Four, her friendship with Kevin, which was placed on hold. Beyond an occasional brief visit with him or the Lees, there wasn't much in Rosemary's life except coming home to Arthur and Gretchen and her books. Arthur did the housework and trained Gretchen, and beyond that there wasn't much in his life except Rosemary.

For a month this routine sustained Rosemary and Arthur. They both moved dutifully through the neatly choreographed steps, never realizing how neutral their lives had become. There were no crises, no upsets, no highs, no lows—just a grinding, boring, seasonless existence that they both passively accepted as "life-after-Della."

This might have gone on indefinitely, but one Monday in mid-November Jackson jolted Rosemary out of her robot routine with a news flash.

"Hey, Rosemary, there is going to be a job opening at the copy center. Shirley and I have been trying to do Kee's work when he's at nightschool, but it's too much. We have our own work to get done. Uncle says he might consider hiring someone for Wednesday and Thursday nights. I told him you had asked about a job. Are you still interested?"

"Am I interested! Am I interested? Jackson, I'm so interested in a job that takes me into the world of the living for two nights a week that I'd sweep floors and wash windows for your uncle."

"My cousin Theodore already has that job—he's twelve," Jackson replied, taking Rosemary's exaggeration seriously. "This job requires more skill."

"Oh, I can handle it, Jackson. I'll learn it quickly. I know I will. Is your uncle hesitating because he thinks I don't know enough?"

"I don't know what the word 'hesitating' means," Jackson said.

"It means holding back."

"No, Uncle is not hesitating for that reason. He's hesitating because the shop is not in a very safe part of town."

"But if I can drive Grandpa's car, I can park right in front of the copy center, can't I? And we all would be leaving at the same time, wouldn't we? So I'd be fine. See?"

"Yes, I will tell Uncle all that," Jackson replied.

"I'll meet you at lunchtime tomorrow," Rosemary planned, "and you can tell me what he says, okay? Thanks, Jackson, thanks a lot."

Rosemary let her hopes soar, totally ignoring the obstacles that might lie in the way of her taking a weeknight job. For the moment, she was alive again, with a shiny new dream.

ॐ Chapter 19 ॐ

Buoyed up by her hopes for a job, Rosemary moved through Tuesday morning with enthusiasm.

At breakfast Arthur commented, "You're certainly cheerful this morning."

"Uh huh," Rosemary responded with a mysterious little smile. "It's a beautiful day, isn't it?"

At school, when she saw Kevin between periods, he asked, "How come you're in such a good mood?"

Rosemary shrugged her shoulders and grinned. "It's just a good morning, I guess."

At lunchtime, when Rosemary saw Shirley at her locker, her greeting was, "It is nice to see you so smiling."

By then Rosemary was detecting a pattern. I must have been pretty grim before, she decided.

Rosemary had only one interest at the moment, however, and that was finding out from Jackson what his uncle had said.

"Jackson will be here . . ." Shirley started to say, when she saw him coming down the hall.

Rosemary went into a brief panic. Can I just ask him straight out, she wondered, or do I have to go through some polite small talk first?

Jackson answered the question by shouting the good news to her while he was still twenty feet away.

"I think there is a job for you."

Rosemary heard the words echoing in her head, but they didn't seem real.

"Say that again, Jackson. Slowly, please."

Jackson said it again, slowly and simply, mouthing each sound and gesturing for emphasis.

"You, Rosemary . . . me, Jackson . . . her, Shirley . . . work together at the copy center."

"It's okay to talk faster if you want, Jackson. I understand English."

Jackson roared with laughter and rattled off the repeat of his news bulletin.

"Hey, great! You told your uncle about me? What did you say?"

Jackson's eyes twinkled, but he kept a straight face. "I told him I knew a terrific young woman who's dependable and follows orders and learns fast. A perfect human being."

"And what did your uncle say?"

"He said, 'If she's that good, I can't afford her!' "

"Is that the end of the story?" Rosemary was amused, but getting nervous, too.

"Next my uncle said, 'Find me someone who's only a little dependable and a little smart who'll work for the kind of money I pay.'"

"So then what did you say?" Rosemary was dying of suspense.

"I said, 'Okay, Uncle, in that case I know a girl named Rosemary Magnuson . . .'"

This time Rosemary was laughing, but she urged Jackson to go on.

"I said, 'This girl might be willing to work for you on Wednesday and Thursday nights when Kee's at his night-school classes.'"

"And . . . ?"

"And Uncle said, 'Have her come to the shop and let Ben decide.'"

"Terrific. When? And who's Ben, by the way?"

"Ben manages the shop for Uncle. He's very busy on a job to be delivered at noon tomorrow, so he cannot see you today. How about tomorrow after school?" Jackson looked at Rosemary, expecting her to be overjoyed. Instead, her expression was clouding over. "What's the matter?" he asked.

"One small detail—I've still got to talk Grandpa into it. He doesn't want me working. He thinks I should be doing homework on school nights."

"Start talking to him tonight," Jackson suggested, "and maybe he'll agree by morning. He can think during the night."

"And maybe he won't agree at all," Rosemary replied gloomily. "Grandpa's really a nice guy, but when he's made up his mind about what's right and what's wrong, he doesn't change it."

"Our father is like that, too," Shirley said. "Only he says the opposite. 'We all must work or we won't be able to survive in America. Work comes first, homework comes second.'"

"And where does sleeping come in?" Rosemary asked. "Third, along with eating?"

"That's right—that's how it is," Jackson agreed.

As they talked, they were walking to the cafeteria.

"How come your uncle isn't hiring one of his relatives?" Rosemary wanted to know. "Why would he consider me?"

"All our relatives who are old enough to work have jobs now," Jackson explained. "That's why Ben has no one to work when Kee's not there."

"Are Ben and Kee your relatives, too?"

"Oh, yes. Everyone at the shop is a relative," Jackson replied. "But some are not close, I guess you say—faraway relatives."

They stopped talking long enough to go through the food service line and to find a table, then Rosemary reopened the subject.

"I really need that job," she confessed. "I'm beginning to die without something else in my life besides schoolwork and long quiet evenings at home with Grandpa."

Shirley shot a reproachful look at Rosemary. "Grandfathers are to be honored."

"I honor him, Shirley. Believe me, I honor him." Rosemary

rushed to her own defense. "And I take care of him, too. But I'm almost seventeen, and I need to feel that I'm able to work as an adult and earn money." She looked at Jackson and Shirley, her eyes pleading for understanding. "I have to do something on my own, not just be someone's granddaughter."

"I understand." Jackson's tone had quickly changed to compassion. He paused, lost in thought. "Would it help . . ." He was thinking out loud. "Would it make any difference if your grandfather met me and we talked together about the job?"

"I don't know, but it's worth a try."

"Maybe I could go to work a little later today and stop at your home first," Jackson suggested. He turned quickly to Shirley. "Could you get that job for the Town and Country Garden Center done for me if I come in late today, Shirley?"

"I think so."

"I could save you some time," Rosemary said, "if I could borrow Grandpa's car and drive you to the copy center after you talk to him." She brightened for a moment. "And maybe, just maybe, he'll have said yes, and I might even see Ben for a moment and make a good impression on him, and . . ." Rosemary was drifting off into the maybe's.

"I'll phone Ben and tell him I'll be a little late," Jackson said.

By the time Rosemary and Jackson finished their planning, the lunch period was over. Agreeing to meet after school at Rosemary's locker, they dashed off to their sixth-period classes.

During the last two periods of the day, Rosemary tested out different strategies in her mind, hoping to hit upon one that would be surefire. No matter how she planned it, she felt doubtful, at best.

On the way home Jackson filled her in on the details of the job. "The hours are five-thirty to nine-thirty, Wednesdays and Thursdays."

"Great!" Rosemary was overjoyed. "I could do my homework fast, eat dinner with Grandpa, and drive his car to work."

"Some of the work is in the back room, and some is at the counter," Jackson explained.

"So I'd be learning to use some of that good equipment?" Rosemary liked that feature.

"Yes, you would."

"And handling money, too?"

"Yes, that too."

"And dealing with the public?"

"That sometimes is the most difficult part of the job. And you also would do layouts and pasteups."

"I'd be learning some real printer's work, wouldn't I?"

"That's right."

"Be sure to emphasize that fact to Grandpa, Jackson. Remember that he's a retired printer."

"What does the word 'emphasize' mean?" Jackson asked.

"To talk about it a lot. To say it over and over. Just keep telling him that I'd be learning the printing trade."

"Okay," Jackson said agreeably. "Learning the trade and earning money while you are learning. That's what I will emphasize."

"You got it. But let's ease into the part about me slowly," Rosemary warned. "Let's talk a lot about the print and copy center first before we hit him with the news."

When they reached the house, Rosemary opened the front door and ushered Jackson into the living room. Arthur was sitting in the arm chair with Gretchen snoozing on his lap.

"Grandpa, this is Jackson Lee," Rosemary said.

"How do you do, Jackson." Arthur held out his hand. "You'll excuse me if I don't get up? Gretchen is exhausted from playing tag with the birds. Sit down, won't you?"

"Want a soda?" Rosemary asked Jackson.

"That sounds good, Rosemary."

"And you, Grandpa?"

"Yes, please."

Rosemary disappeared into the kitchen, chuckling over the surprised look on her grandfather's face. He covered it up fairly well, but she knew he was bursting with curiosity about the young man she had brought home. She hurried back to rescue Jackson if he needed it, bringing three sodas and a box of crackers with her. Let's try to keep the situation as relaxed as possible, she kept thinking nervously as she passed the refreshments to Arthur and Jackson.

"Grandpa, Jackson is learning to be a printer, so I thought you would enjoy meeting him. He works at the print and copy center on Lincoln Street. His uncle owns it."

"Is that right?" Arthur came alive. "I'm a retired printer. In fact, I owned my own shop for thirty years."

"That's wonderful, Mr. Magnuson." Jackson responded enthusiastically. "I hope someday I can own a shop. I like the business."

"You know, I came to America when I was about your age,

Jackson, and I started as a printer's helper just like you're doing. Have you been in America a long time?"

"Oh no, I have only been here since September."

"But you speak English so well . . ."

"Rosemary has been teaching English to me and my sister, Shirley, at lunchtime."

"You never mentioned this, Rosemary."

"You and I got busy with other things, Grandpa. But look how fast he learns. Jackson and Shirley are very smart people. They are great with high-tech equipment, and that shop has a lot of it."

"Oh, do you use the new . . . ?" Arthur and Jackson plunged into an animated discussion of all the new developments in printing equipment. Rosemary watched them toss questions and answers back and forth, her head swiveling like a spectator's at a tennis match.

Suddenly Arthur paused and started off in another direction. "But what kind of building security do you have, Jackson? Your shop is a likely target for robberies, with Lincoln Street so dark."

"Oh, we have a good security system, Mr. Magnuson. We've installed silent alarms in many locations, and they are tied in with the police. We are friends with the police—they check on us regularly at night. It's quite safe working there."

Rosemary's heart had been racing and her throat tightening until Jackson gave his final reassurance. But even with that, she could sense Arthur thinking that he wouldn't want *his* family working there at night.

Apprehensively, Rosemary eased the subject around to the Wednesday-Thursday job. "Grandpa, Ben needs someone to cover for Kee on the two evenings he goes to night school. Jackson thinks I could get the job."

A look of apprehension came over Arthur's face.

"It's only from five-thirty to nine-thirty on Wednesday and Thursday." She was racing through all the good points. "I could get my homework done, have dinner with you, and be home before ten. It's perfect, Grandpa."

Rosemary knew when she said it that Arthur did not think it was perfect at all, or even halfway acceptable.

"Could I see about the job, Grandpa?"

"She could be earning money while she's learning the trade." Jackson dutifully slipped in his pitch.

Rosemary's heart was pounding. She could hear the no even before Arthur said it.

"I honestly feel that you need your week nights at home, Rosemary," Arthur said solemnly, "but I hate being the bad guy in this situation. If Ben has a Saturday opening, I would approve, but I can't say yes to the weeknight job."

Rosemary's face fell. She was too stunned and hurt to protest. "Can I use the car to take Jackson to work?" she asked abruptly.

"Of course. It's been a pleasure meeting you, Jackson. Come again, please."

"Thank you," Jackson replied. "Good-bye."

Rosemary was numb. For a while she drove in silence. At last Jackson observed quietly, "When the grandfather says no, there is nothing more to be said."

"It's not fair."

"But the decision is made." Jackson could see that Rosemary was very unhappy. "I'll see if Uncle needs Saturday help. It's been very busy on Saturdays."

Rosemary just nodded and drove on without replying. When she stopped in front of the copy center, Jackson thanked her and got out. With a limp wave as her only response, Rosemary gunned the engine and sped off.

Her driving was terrible. The hurt and frustration building up in her were reflected in squealing brakes, jerky stops and starts, and a lot of honking. She screeched to a stop in front of her house, anger replacing the early hurt.

With the car put away in the garage, Rosemary stalked into the house, ignored her grandfather in the kitchen, and ceremoniously locked herself in her room. After flinging a few pillows around and pounding the mattress with her fists, Rosemary stretched out on her bed and seethed.

That's the stupidest thing I ever heard of, she fumed. Totally unfair. No good reason to say no. What's he trying to do to me?

Rosemary's eyes narrowed suspiciously. What is he trying to do? Is he going to try to keep me a little girl, always in his care, so I won't grow up and leave him alone?

The minute Rosemary thought of that possibility, she clapped a hand over her mouth guiltily. What an awful thought about a person like Grandpa! But he's being unreasonable about this simple little request. Rosemary went back to her anger.

She had been nursing it along for an hour when there was a knock on her door.

"Dinner's ready," Arthur called.

"I'm not hungry," Rosemary replied, without opening the door. She said nothing more, hoping the silent treatment would affect Arthur.

Without doing any reflective thinking, Rosemary remained locked in her room until nine-thirty. It was dark outside and dark in her room, and her anger and fury had turned into self-pity. She could hear movement in the house. Arthur had long since finished in the kitchen and had watched some TV shows. The scurrying of Gretchen's paws in the hallway indicated that she was having one last romp before bedtime.

Rosemary began to feel abandoned and left out. Her self-exile was backfiring. Listen to them, she told herself indignantly. Grandpa really *is* going to bed. She heard him calling Gretchen to come and settle down. Soon the lights clicked off.

Rosemary's heart sank. She was all alone with her own bad temper in a darkened house. Slowly and quietly, she opened her door to peek. It was true, just as she thought. The whole house was silent and dark. Rosemary closed her door quietly and undressed in the darkness. Lonely and miserable, she crawled into bed and hugged Benjamin Bear.

She lay in the darkness for a long time. Too many things were unresolved for her to have any hope of sleeping. Then she heard movement, Arthur's slippers going into the bathroom, and, yes, they were coming toward Rosemary's room. She could sense her grandfather's presence outside her door. The doorknob turned. The door opened. Arthur inched his way toward Rosemary's bed and felt for a place to sit.

"Rosemary," Arthur whispered, "I've been considering very

carefully, and I'm going to change my decision. Not because I think the original one was wrong, mind you. I'm changing it because you seem to feel that I'm hurting you again. You've had too many hurts recently, and I don't want to inflict any more pain on you." Arthur sighed deeply. "You may go ahead and apply for the job."

"Oh, Grandpa!" In the darkness Rosemary groped for her grandfather's open arms. "I don't deserve it," she sobbed. "What makes me act like an adult one time and then turn right around and act like a spoiled kid the next?" Rosemary wiped her eyes on her pillowcase.

"It's called growing up," Arthur replied. His hands were trembling and his voice choking. "I saw your mother through it—I'll see you through it. And down the road, Rosemary, when you have children someday, I hope you'll be patient in seeing them through it."

"Oh, Gramp . . ."

Arthur held his granddaughter in his arms for a moment. "Want some dinner now?" he asked softly.

"I'm starved," Rosemary replied.

"I held it for you. Let's go get it," Arthur urged.

They blinked in the bright light of the kitchen and smiled shyly at each other. While Rosemary wolfed down the long-delayed dinner, Arthur reminisced about his coming to America like Jackson, and learning English like Jackson, and starting out in the printing trade like Jackson.

Finally, Arthur paused and withdrew into some private thoughts. When he emerged, he assumed his most casual manner to ask the next question. "Is there more between you and Jackson than a job at the copy center?" He tried not to look embarrassed by the question.

"Yes, Grandpa. Lots more." Rosemary wasn't going to let Arthur off easy.

"Lots more? You mean this has been going on under my nose, and I've been unaware and uninformed?" Arthur shook his head in dismay. "I need Della to keep me up on such things. Just exactly what's between you and Jackson?"

"Oh, Grandpa, quit sounding like my caretaker. I think I'm old enough to handle my life."

"That's what scares me!"

"All right." Rosemary weakened. She had already put her grandfather through enough stress for one day. "What's between us is friendship. Kevin introduced me to Jackson and his sister, Shirley, on their first day in an American school, and we liked each other right from the start. It's plain and simple, Gramp. Friendship. And Shirley has become a special friend, as Cynthia's always been. We both love to sew, and, for her birthday, I think I'm going to start her on a teddy bear collection."

Arthur hesitated and cleared his throat before tossing out the next question. "Just to clarify things for an old man, Rosemary, is your friendship with Kevin also classified as plain and simple?"

Rosemary knew her grandfather was angling for a hint that would show Kevin had an edge.

"No, Gramp." Her response was guarded. "I'd call that one complicated."

With a twinkle in her eye indicating that the subject was

closed, Rosemary got up and put the milk carton in the refrigerator. "Thanks for being so great, Gramp."

"Well, tonight is one of my better times," Arthur said, his expression knowing. "You'll notice that we all have our good moments and we all have our bad moments. We can afford to forgive another person's bad times because we never know when we'll be in that position ourselves."

"Oh, quit being so wise, Gramp. Get some sleep. Maybe it'll go away by morning." Rosemary poked Arthur playfully, and he grinned back.

Gretchen's tail flapped back and forth between them, her sign of relief that peace had been restored to her small world.

✑ Chapter 20 ✐

Rosemary's overriding concern on Wednesday was the forthcoming job interview. She carefully chose an outfit that would look grown-up and businesslike, but still not be too conspicuous at school. She dressed with care, then rechecked her hair, her nails, her smile. While she fixed and ate breakfast, she listened attentively to Arthur's briefing on the essential things a prospective employee of a printing firm should know. And then she put in seven totally wasted hours at school. Education had no significance whatever for Rosemary that day, except as a filler between breakfast and her job interview.

After school, as Rosemary walked with Shirley and Jackson to the copy center, she was all nerves. Shirley patiently reassured her, but Rosemary was certain she would somehow blow the whole thing.

"I'm telling you," Jackson said as they turned onto the last block, "you'll be fine—you're just what he wants."

"I'm not as good with machines as you are," Rosemary argued.

"But you speak better English," Jackson argued back.

"Yeah, but are they English-speaking machines?"

"No, they're Japanese! We both lose."

Jackson's infectious chuckle had Rosemary laughing as she entered the copy center and was introduced to Ben.

After having worried so much in advance, she found Ben's interview unnervingly casual.

"Jackson and Shirley seem to think you can handle the job," Ben said.

"I'll have to learn it, but I'm a fast learner," Rosemary replied.

"If they say you're okay, I'm satisfied. Can you start tomorrow?"

"Sure."

"See you at five-thirty tomorrow, then." Ben picked up some papers from his desk and disappeared into the back room. Surprised that it was all over, Rosemary looked around for Jackson and Shirley. She spotted both of them at a work station in the corner.

"What do you know!" she whispered as she detoured past the Lees on the way to the door. "I start tomorrow."

"Wonderful!" Shirley beamed.

"That's great," Jackson whispered back. "We really need someone terrific who's dependable and follows orders and learns fast."

"But you'll settle for me. I know!" Rosemary grinned back at Jackson as she left.

Elated over her triumph, Rosemary hurried home to tell the good news to her grandfather. If Arthur had any earlier doubts about the reversal of his decision, they were quickly dispelled by an evening of Rosemary's buoyant spirits.

The next morning Arthur watched his granddaughter leave for school, humming cheerfully. Seven hours later he saw her return home, still in high spirits. After polishing off all her homework in a short time, Rosemary carried on an animated and interesting dinner conversation for a change.

I'd forgotten what a job can do for a young person's morale, Arthur mused. It never occurred to me that a job for Rosemary would make my own life so much more pleasant.

As Rosemary drove away at five-fifteen, Arthur found himself wiping away a tear as a wave of nostalgia engulfed him. Silently wishing his granddaughter success and safety in her printing venture, he turned to Gretchen and stroked her head.

Ben was ready to leave for the day when Rosemary arrived for work. "Shirley and Jackson and Curtis will all be here to show you what to do," he told her. "You'll learn the routine quickly."

Ben left the shop and Curtis took over the orientation, starting immediately with lesson one: the security system.

"We have buttons that silently call the police," he told Rosemary. "Follow me and learn where the buttons are located."

Rosemary chuckled to herself. Grandpa went over the basics of printing with me, she thought, but he forgot lesson one. Apparently, the first thing to know about printing, if you're working on Lincoln Street at night, is how to stay alive in a holdup. These days we have fire drills, earthquake drills, and holdup drills—all the little precautionary routines.

"Now, when you use the alarm system," Curtis continued, "just keep calm until the police arrive. They are friendly to us and can arrive very quickly. The police station is only three blocks away."

Rosemary rolled her eyes upward. "You really are used to routine holdups!"

"In this neighborhood you more or less expect them." Curtis was philosophical in the face of this irony.

"Now, here's how you . . ." Finished with security, he launched into the full training program. "You can start with this work tonight." Curtis set Rosemary up at a work station in a little cubicle just behind the front counter.

Shirley was working on a big job in the back room with the door closed, and Jackson was moving back and forth from the counter and cash register to the copy machines that the public used. For a while there was a flurry of evening customers, but finally it leveled off. By eight forty-five, as dusk gave way to darkness, the customers were all gone, and Jackson and Rosemary were finally able to concentrate on their work without interruptions.

Curtis looked at the clock and pulled out his metal lunch pail. Rosemary watched the routine from her cubicle, fascinated. It was like a carefully choreographed dance. Curtis opened the pail and set it on a low stool behind the counter. He filled a canvas bag with the money from the cash register and the contents of the safe. Instead of taking a thermos and some sandwiches from the lunch pail, he put the canvas bag into the pail. Next, he fastened a little padlock on his "lunch" and hid the key in his shoe. Finally, he put on an old tattered jacket and a funny knit ski cap. Curtis, who a moment before had looked like a well-dressed Asian-American businessman, was instantly transformed into a tired workman returning home with his empty lunch pail after a long day on the job.

"Carry on while I'm gone," Curtis called as he went out the door.

Jackson turned to Rosemary. "Every evening he takes the money to the night deposit at the bank," he explained. "He doesn't draw much attention looking like that."

"No one's likely to mug him to get his beat-up lunch pail," Rosemary agreed. "I just don't believe it, the way all the bases are covered. You've thought of everything."

Jackson laughed. "When you work nights on Lincoln Street, it helps to be smart."

Rosemary sensed that his laughter masked something much deeper, but Jackson turned his attention to a stack of papers at the front counter.

A few minutes later, Rosemary glanced up from her work and saw a shabbily dressed man get out of a car and stand next to the parking meter outside the shop. She felt uneasy, even though it was a public sidewalk and the man was only standing there. But just in case, Rosemary reviewed in her mind the locations of all the security alarm buttons. There wasn't one in the cubicle where she was working, but there was a foot-controlled button near Jackson.

Rosemary became more nervous as the man stepped into the

light of the doorway. He looked up the street and down the street before turning to enter the shop.

Uh oh, Rosemary thought grimly, it's Jackson's turn tonight.

The man walked over to the counter and stood opposite Jackson, one hand in his pocket, his eyes nervously scanning the shop. Rosemary stirred, and the man quickly turned to stare at her.

"May I help you?" Jackson asked in a calm voice.

The man's hand moved in his pocket.

This is it, Rosemary thought. He's going to pull a gun on Jackson. What do I do? Curtis's careful instructions melted together in her mind, but she remained still, sensing that any movement might cause the man to react irrationally.

"Uh . . . I just . . ."

He's stalling, Rosemary thought. Why isn't Jackson reaching for the floor button?

". . . want one copy of this." The man pulled a folded and frayed paper from his pocket. "But it looks like you only do big jobs here." He refolded the paper and started to return it to his pocket.

"Our big machines can do little jobs," Jackson replied. He held out his hand for the sheet. "Here, I'll do it for you."

Still unable to accept the man as a simple, nervous customer, Rosemary remained frozen while the big machine whirred and stopped, and Jackson handed the man his fresh copy and the tattered original.

"There you are, sir."

Rosemary's stomach fluttered as the man's hand plunged into his pocket and came up with a dollar bill.

"The big machines only look tricky," Jackson added with a smile as he made change.

The man folded his new copy, slipped it into his pocket, and hurried out of the shop. As his car pulled away from the curb, Jackson turned to make a routine comment, then paused to stare at Rosemary with concern.

"Rosemary, you look like a . . ." Jackson gestured and groped for the word. "White, like a . . ."

"Ghost," Rosemary prompted. "White like a ghost."

"What's the matter? Are you okay?"

"Just a victim of the security drills." Rosemary dropped onto a chair, limp and laughing nervously. "I thought it was going to be a holdup. When he had his hand in his pocket, I was sure he . . ."

Shirley, hearing raised voices, peeked through the doorway. "What's happening?"

Feeling silly, but relieved, Rosemary replayed the incident for Shirley, carefully including all the misread signals. They were still recalling new details when Curtis returned from the bank. Between their outbursts of laughter, they tried to tell him what he had missed. Curtis couldn't do anything but join in the laughter.

With a relaxed feeling of comradeship, they closed the shop for the night, setting the security alarm system on automatic and locking the doors securely. Curtis, Jackson, and Shirley drove off in one direction and Rosemary in the other.

Rosemary was so wound up as she headed home that she wondered how she would ever get to sleep. Wait till I tell the story to Grandpa. He'll . . . oh no, I can't let him know holdups are considered routine where I work. He'll be afraid to let me go back.

She parked the car in the garage and opened the door slowly. Arthur and Gretchen were dozing in the armchair, waiting to greet her before going to bed.

"They must have put you right to work," Arthur said, blinking to wake up and look alert. He squinted at Rosemary. "Your cheeks are flushed and you look so alive," he commented. "It must be a very challenging job."

"Oh, it is, Grandpa. It is. It takes even more talents than you told me. You'd never believe what it takes."

"I'd believe it," Arthur replied. "And you think tonight was challenging—wait till the night some guy comes in with a gun in his pocket and tells you to empty the cash register into his bag. Now there's an evening in a print shop that will make the adrenalin flow."

"Yeah, that I gotta see," Rosemary agreed. "That I gotta see."

"Come on and tell me about the shop while we have a cup of hot chocolate," Arthur suggested. He was anxious to fix a snack for his granddaughter. This was something Della always did if Rosemary had been out in the evening, and Arthur knew it was one of the little touches that Rosemary missed.

With a polite apology to Gretchen, Arthur lifted the small dog off his lap so he could stand up. She followed closely at his heels, confident that there would be a treat for her in the kitchen. Rosemary followed, too, wanting to encourage her grandfather's return to sociability.

Straddling the kitchen chair, Rosemary rested her chin on

the back of it and watched Arthur preparing the chocolate. With a smile of satisfaction, he soon placed a steaming mug in front of his granddaughter and sat down to visit.

Rosemary was amazed to see Arthur so animated. He had been subdued and depressed for such a long time that she had forgotten how sparkling her grandfather could be when he was himself. She would have loved to laugh with him about her silly dramatic scene, but she carefully steered away from that subject, knowing that if Arthur feared for her safety, it would be the end of her job. They talked, instead, about printing and copying equipment, and customers, although Rosemary did spice up the technical talk with the story about Curtis's ingenious banking procedures. That night they went to bed in a different mood. It seemed as if one layer of the despair that covered their household had been lifted.

As Rosemary turned out the lights and settled into her bed, she was still chuckling to herself about how she had misread the situation. In the dark, however, the humor rapidly faded as the real possibilities began to register. The security measures at the copy center had been set up in response to known dangers. There could have been a real gun in the man's pocket. The real gun could have been pointed right at Jackson, and if the real gunman had got mad or impatient or even a little nervous, well . . .

Thinking about it made Rosemary sick. She began to tremble, knowing how easily she could have been on the very brink of a disaster. The next time it might not be funny—it might be horrible. Jackson, or anyone else in the shop, could become an instant victim. Working nights in a shop on a dark city street had built-in hazards.

Slowly Rosemary began to understand that the owners and employees of the print and copy center knew they were at risk. They couldn't change that reality. But instead of surrendering their right to do business, they devised smart ways to protect themselves. Greatly sobered, she finally came to respectful terms with the dangers of the job and dropped off to sleep.

❧ Chapter 21 ❧

Rosemary awoke in the morning feeling vaguely good. It took her a while to figure out what there was to celebrate, but eventually her thinking came around to the priorities she had set during her soul-searching day on the ridge trail. She counted them off on her fingers. Number One—get caught up on schoolwork. Done. Number Two—divide up the household chores. Done. Number Three—get the job at the copy center. Done. Yay, I'm practically home free. No wonder I feel good, she thought.

Number Four—take better care of my special friendship with Kevin. Rosemary knew that there was more to that resolution, something she had never dared to voice. Now she risked it, putting it into words very tentatively. Take better care of my special friendship with Kevin and perhaps let it grow into something more. She shivered nervously. I think there have been signs. Yes, I know there have been, but I haven't acknowledged them.

I've been busy, she thought defensively, very busy getting Priorities One, Two, and Three under control.

A nagging little voice wouldn't let Rosemary accept this new thought.

So, now that the first three priorities are in order, what's your excuse? Go on, what's your excuse now?

I'm still very busy. I've got Grandpa, and my schoolwork, and my new job.

And?

And I don't really know. I guess I just can't see Kevin in another role. He's been the kid down the block for so long. I guess I don't see him as an adult.

Was he a kid when your grandmother died? Was he a kid when your grandfather had to be rushed to the emergency room?

No . . . no, he acted a lot more mature than I did. Yeah, okay, so I owe him a lot.

Better not think that way, the little voice cautioned. Don't try to do that young man any favors, tossing him a crumb of attention in order to pay your debts. Besides, now that Kevin is becoming an adult, he might possibly have someone else in mind to play that other role with, someone quite different from the girl down the block. Has that possibility occurred to you?

Rosemary was taken aback. That's fighting dirty, she told the little voice angrily. I'm special to him . . . I think I am. He really cares for me . . . he does . . . I think . . .

Well, good luck. You're never going to find out, the way you're going.

The little voice was through, and Rosemary was left with some sobering self-doubts that she would have to carry to school with her, because it was time to get moving.

Rosemary put the heavy thinking aside as she left the house. It wasn't getting her anywhere.

Kevin happened to be leaving Muirwood Way just ahead of her. Shall I call him or let him go on alone? she wondered. Before her conscience could start nagging again, she settled the issue by yelling, "Hey, Kevin!"

Kevin turned around, greeting Rosemary with a friendly wave, and waited for her to catch up.

"I haven't seen you for a while," he said. "Been hiding?"

"No, just trying to catch up. I have a list of four things, and I'm working my way down it."

"Sounds very organized. What's on the list?"

"Get caught up in school, and I've done that. Do my new share of the housework, and I'm doing that. Get a part-time job, and I just got that yesterday. I'll be working Wednesday and Thursday nights at the copy center where Shirley and Jackson work."

"Great. You kind of need that, don't you? A little time away from your grandpa . . . earn some money . . . run your own show."

Rosemary was startled by Kevin's instant understanding of her needs, which she herself had only dimly perceived. "You always seem to have the situation sized up before I tell you what's going on."

Kevin smiled. "So what's Number Four on the list? What's next?"

Rosemary had walked right into that one, unaware that she might expose herself. She groped for an evasive answer. "Uh . . . it's kind of like being more sociable, or something." Knowing the explanation was inadequate, she blushed and looked away.

Kevin sensed Rosemary's discomfort, as well as her lack of disclosure, and changed the subject. "How's your grandfather doing these days?"

"Well . . . he's not in the terrible shape he was in before we got Gretchen."

Kevin detected something unfinished in her assessment. "But?"

It took a while for Rosemary to figure out what the "but" really was. Finally she added, "But there's nothing going on in his life."

"Haven't the church friends been around?"

"Not much lately. I guess they figure they got us through the crisis."

"How about the group at the senior center that the doctor said he should get into?"

"I've tried to get him to go, but he doesn't want to. And I can't just take him and enroll him like a child entering school."

Kevin nodded his understanding. "So you're all he has right now."

"Yep."

"And you're not able to be all the things he needs."

"Something like that," Rosemary agreed, adding with resignation, "I don't see any answers."

They were approaching the school, and Kevin didn't want to leave Rosemary on a down note. "Maybe there'll be some surprises," he suggested hopefully.

"I've already had enough of them!"

"Well, let's think about it."

They paused on the front steps of the school before plunging into the crowded hallways. For a moment their eyes met. Slowly Kevin smiled at Rosemary as he left her. She suddenly felt warm all over. Funny, she mused, I never noticed his smile was like that. And his eyes—they didn't used to be so nice. What's happening to him?

Kevin stayed in Rosemary's mind throughout the day. She found herself looking forward to meeting him after school and talking some more on the way home. Their paths didn't cross, however, and Rosemary had to admit reluctantly that the kid who had always been around had somehow slipped through her hands when his company would have been welcome.

She felt a strange sense of loneliness as she trudged toward home. Her eyes searched hopefully for a glimpse of Kevin as she passed his house, but there was no sign of him. Now I may not have a chance to see him again until Monday, she thought wistfully. He's always busy on weekends—does errands for his mother, gone a lot.

Rosemary carried the wistfulness with her all through the evening. As she and Arthur watched their favorite Friday night TV show, she kept experiencing some kind of vague anxiety, feeling as if she were standing on a doorstep waiting for a door to open. It was a new feeling, hard to identify. Rosemary could not decide whether it felt good or bad. She drifted off into sleep, still wondering.

ꙅ Chapter 22 ꙅ

Saturday morning dawned crisp and clear. Rosemary threw back her blankets and shivered in surprise. The house had got chilly during the night. An autumn tang was in the air. Retreating again to the warmth of her blankets, she lay in bed, enjoying the luxury of a free morning. Through her window she could see the liquid amber tree, her own unofficial indicator of shifting seasons. Without her noticing, its leaves had turned red and then shriveled and dropped, leaving a bony skeleton for the winter. The feeding station, hanging from a long outstretched branch, which served flocks of birds in the summer, now accommodated only a handful of winter residents.

As Rosemary gazed through the window, two brilliant leaves floated gracefully to the ground. I'll bet that whole corner is an untidy mess now, she thought. I'm going to have to do some yard cleanup soon. In fact, I'll start on the chrysanthemums this morning, she decided. The ones by the front door have got ragged. The fact that Kevin's house was clearly visible from the front yard had something to do with Rosemary's decision.

"I'm going to clean up the front flower bed," she announced right after breakfast.

"That will be a big help," Arthur replied. "I just haven't had the heart to do anything with Della's plants yet."

"I'll do it."

Rosemary took the clippers and stepped out into the fresh November morning. As she trimmed the dead blossoms from the chrysanthemum plants, she kept glancing toward Kevin's house.

As if in answer to some psychic message, Kevin suddenly appeared on his doorstep.

"Hey, Rosie," he called. "I was just coming to see you."

Kevin's voice brought Rosemary to life. She waved and watched him as he ran the block. His dark hair moved softly with each step, but the unruly front lock rose and fell.

"I've got an idea!"

Kevin was out of breath when he reached Rosemary. His cheeks were glowing; his eyes sparkled with excitement.

"See what you think of this one."

I like it, Rosemary thought before she even heard what it was. I like it. Just keep talking, Kevin. I like it.

"Come on inside and tell me," she urged.

"No, we'd better talk out here where your grandfather can't hear."

"Oh—okay, what's so secret?"

They sat down on the curb.

"See if this isn't tailor-made for your grandfather." Kevin could hardly contain his enthusiasm. "I just found out that the SPCA runs a Hug-a-Pet program. People volunteer to take their pets to visit nursing homes each week and let the patients hold the animals and talk to them. Wouldn't Gretchen be a natural for that job? And wouldn't your grandpa get a lift from helping people by sharing Gretchen with them?"

"What an angle! You're right, Kev." The idea caught Rosemary's fancy. "It sure sounds like what he needs." Suddenly her face fell. "But he might brush off the suggestion just like he did the senior center idea—and once he says no, that's it."

Rosemary glanced at Kevin. He was full of hope, refusing to hear any doubts. "On the other hand," she continued, "if you were the one to tell him about it, Kevin, I'll bet he'd take it seriously. You know how he feels about you!"

"True blue . . ." Kevin started.

"Through and through," Rosemary completed. "Come on, you could sell him anything." She took Kevin's hand and led him up the walk. "Watch, he'll be in the front room holding Gretchen," she whispered as she put her hand on the doorknob. "All right, now do your stuff, Kevin."

Arthur was surprised to see Kevin, but his sense of courtesy brought him quickly to his feet, unseating Gretchen in the process. For a moment the little dog was confused, but soon she went straight to Kevin, planting herself beside the visitor, wagging her tail and watching him intently.

Kevin reached down to stroke Gretchen. "You are a charmer, Gretchen." He held the furry face in his hands and looked into the dark eyes. "You really know how to make people feel good, don't you?"

Kevin turned to Arthur. "Gretchen's so well trained, Mr. Magnuson, her manners are better than most people's."

"Yes, Gretchen does know how to behave," Arthur admitted proudly. "We've worked a lot on that. She loves to show off."

Grandpa is falling right into the trap, Rosemary thought.

"She'd be great with elderly shut-ins, wouldn't she?" Kevin continued.

"Oh yes, she loves attention and she's very gentle," Arthur agreed, not knowing that the trap was almost ready to spring.

"Mr. Magnuson," Kevin said in his most persuasive tone, "why don't you enroll Gretchen in the SPCA Hug-a-Pet program where she could bring happiness to nursing home patients every week? She'd be so great at it."

"The Hug-a-What program?" Arthur looked confused.

"Hug-a-Pet."

"Oh, I wouldn't want her out of my care, Kevin. That's impossible. She's too young to be away from me."

"But you would be the one who took her to the people for hugging."

Arthur was lost in thought. "I don't think I'd be any good at that sort of thing," he finally replied. "I'm a printer by trade. I've never worked much with people, especially sick or elderly ones."

"That's okay, Mr. Magnuson." Kevin was closing in.

"Gretchen knows all that stuff. You just have to know how to handle Gretchen, that's all." He looked at Arthur for a reaction. "And you already know that," he added, with a casual shrug of his shoulders.

"She's well trained," Arthur agreed with obvious pride. "Yes, I'd say she's a human relations expert."

"That's right." Kevin was ready to fire his final round. "With all her talent, you wouldn't want to deny Gretchen a fulfilling career of helping people, would you?"

Arthur squinted at Kevin and exploded with laughter. Gretchen rushed to his side, nervously trying to decide whether everything was all right. Arthur put his hand under her chin and spoke very softly to the dog.

"Little lady, do you feel the need to become a career woman? Am I preventing you from a fulfilling life of social service? Kevin seems to think you should be doing something more than being a man's home companion."

Gretchen was blossoming under all the attention. Arthur wasn't doing badly, either. He was happily succumbing to Kevin's persuasive charms.

"What's involved in all this, Kevin?" Arthur asked.

"Well, first Gretchen would have two sessions of behavioral screening. Then you yourself would have several training classes in the use of pets with the elderly. After that you would choose which nursing homes you and Gretchen would visit on a regular basis. The SPCA would set it all up, and the patients would be alerted to start looking forward to Gretchen's visits—and yours."

"I must say, Kevin, it's not something I ever would have thought of doing. But I might consider it for Gretchen's benefit. Life with an old man is just too dull for a bouncy young thing."

"Yeah," Rosemary pitched in, "she needs to go dancing and things."

Arthur turned to his granddaughter with a save-the-comments look and replied with dignity to Kevin.

"Thank you, Kevin. For Gretchen's sake I'll consider your suggestion. I appreciate your concern."

"Sure, Mr. Magnuson. You know the phone number of the SPCA, I'm sure."

"Just ask Gretchen, if you forget," Rosemary said.

Kevin shot Rosemary a glance that told her not to come out with any other bright observations that might distract her grandfather.

"I have to be going," he said, with a smile for Arthur.

Arthur had risen to say good-bye. "It's always good to see you, Kevin. Drop by again—soon."

Rosemary walked out to the sidewalk with Kevin. "I don't believe it," she kept murmuring. "How do you do it?"

"Your grandfather's an old softie," he told Rosemary. "Just a marshmallow. You know that, don't you?"

"I'm learning it," Rosemary admitted. "Now we'll see if he really follows through."

"He will," Kevin predicted. "He's going to do it because he feels it will be good for Gretchen. You watch."

Kevin was right. Arthur did go to the SPCA on Monday.

When Rosemary got home from school, Arthur was brimming with news.

"Gretchen passed the behavioral screening with such high marks that she's excused from the second visit," Arthur announced with pride. "She's fully certified as a Hug-a-Pet."

"How about that!" Rosemary loved seeing her grandfather's eyes sparkle again. "Congratulations, Gretchen. You're some lady!"

"And," Arthur continued, "they were so taken by her that they called their photographer to come in and take pictures of her. They'll be used on their publicity posters for the nursing homes."

"Your furry face will be famous, Gretch," Rosemary whispered to the little dog. "The Hug-a-Pet face."

"And . . ." Arthur paused to size up Rosemary's reaction. "And since the program is just starting, they need an informational brochure to be handed out for publicity, so I told them I'd do the layout and get it printed for them."

Rosemary gave an impressed whistle. "You don't go into things halfway, do you, Gramp! How many days a week did you sign up for?"

"Five days a week, two hours a day."

"That's some career this girl is embarking on."

"She'll bring sunshine and smiles to lots of people that way." Arthur's tone was almost reverent.

Rosemary looked her grandfather straight in the eye. Her joking tone gone. "And so will you, Grandpa. You know that, don't you?"

Arthur looked away in embarrassment. "Oh, I'm just furnishing transportation for the star."

"Right," Rosemary agreed.

"And by the way," Arthur said in an offhand way, "I thought I could work with Jackson and his associates on the printing for the brochure."

"Oh, we'll get you the best," Rosemary promised. "The very best job in town." She looked at Arthur with an amused smile. "And whose picture is going to be on the brochure, Grandpa? Our little fair-haired star, by any chance?"

"Who else?" Arthur avoided Rosemary's eyes.

"Pushy parent, aren't you!" she accused teasingly.

Arthur didn't rise to her bait. "You know—" his mind was racing ahead—"a short TV commercial might be another good way to get public support for the program." He squinted pensively at Gretchen, sizing up her TV potential.

Rosemary studied her grandfather, suddenly so animated and full of ideas. "You know what, Gramp? I really think the publicity should show the Hug-a-Pet team instead of just the pet. GRETCHEN AND GRAMP—THE G-TEAM. Can't you see the poster? TUESDAY AT TWO IN THE LOUNGE—THE G-TEAM."

"Quit thinking so hard." Arthur cautioned. He looked quizzically at Rosemary. "You really think so?"

"As your consultant from your printing firm, I think you need a man and a dog together in your publicity. It would portray the partnership aspect of the operation." Rosemary was startled by how professional she sounded.

"Well, I really can't argue with my printing consultant."

Arthur picked up Gretchen and held her in front of the mirror, striking different poses.

"You're absolutely right," he admitted. "In fact, it's uncanny how right you've been on this whole venture, Rosemary."

"Well," Rosemary confessed, "actually Kevin is the brain behind it."

Arthur acknowledged Kevin's role with a nod and continued trying out various poses with Gretchen.

Rosemary's mind drifted away from the moment. She was remembering the scene when Kevin first introduced the idea of this unlikely crusade to her. Pretty smart, aren't you? she thought. Not bad thinking at all for a kid down the street who can't even handle his own hair. Not bad at all.

ঌ Chapter 23 ঌ

Ever since the death of Della, the Magnuson household had been suspended in a delicate balance. During Arthur's long-sustained depression, Rosemary had been preoccupied with the tricky job of keeping him from total despair. Without realizing it, she was postponing her own adjustment to loss while she struggled valiantly to maintain some family equilibrium.

Now, thanks to Hug-a-Pet, the balance was shifting, and Arthur was on the rising end of the scale. For the first time since his loss of Della, he had something to wake up for each day. He was out of bed at seven every morning, eager to start his grooming and training session with Gretchen. The little dog quickly acquired the airs of a child who knows she's loved. Her eyes danced, her fur glistened, her manners were impeccable. She was ready and eager to bring sunshine to the nursing home world.

Each morning after his session with Gretchen, Arthur would turn his attention to the Hug-a-Pet brochure. He kept the pages spread across the table so he could shift things around and ultimately achieve a perfect layout.

"Do you think this looks better here, Rosemary?" Arthur would slip a photo into an empty spot.

"Yeah, that's fine, Grandpa."

"Or is this better?"

"That's fine, too."

"No, the balance would be better with it like this," Arthur would finally decide.

Actually, a balanced page didn't really matter to Rosemary, but her grandfather's enthusiasm did.

"I think the whole thing is very professional," she said as Arthur meticulously added the finishing touches to the layout. "I'm impressed. You're good, Grandpa. Very good!"

Arthur, feeling satisfied, wrapped up his work, delivered it to the copy center, and settled down to two days of worrying about the outcome of his project.

"Grandpa, relax," Rosemary advised. "The copy center people are going to be very kind to it. They'll handle it gently, speak softly to it, and return your finished brochure by their special messenger service."

Arthur grinned sheepishly at his granddaughter. "It's kind of like awaiting a birth."

"Well, Jackson and Shirley and I are very good birth attendants," Rosemary teased, "so quit worrying."

On Wednesday, when Rosemary was getting ready to leave

for work, Arthur hung around as if he wanted to say something, but didn't know how.

"Got something on your mind?" Rosemary finally asked.

"I have a favor to ask. Would you take a peek at my brochure and see if it's going to look good?"

"Yes, Grandpa, I will."

"Thanks." Arthur sighed. "I know I'm being silly."

"Not really." Rosemary tried to be reassuring. "It matters a lot to you."

"I'll send one to Sigrid to introduce Gretchen to her, and . . ."

As Rosemary drove off, Arthur sat down in the chair by the window, stroking Gretchen's ears and talking to her about the brochure with their picture on the cover.

An hour later he was amazed to look out and find his car at the curb. Rosemary was handing Jackson a package from the trunk. Arthur hurried to open the door.

"Here it is, Grandpa, hand-delivered by your friendly printers." Rosemary looked triumphant. Jackson glowed with pride.

Arthur was flustered and nervous as Jackson ceremoniously opened the package and pulled out a brochure.

"Here you are, Mr. Magnuson," he said. "What do you think? Ben is so proud of this job that he is using it in his sales packet to show customers what fine quality work we do."

"Oh my!" Arthur studied the brochure silently. "Won't Sigrid love that?" He held it up for a different viewing angle. "It's even better than I hoped. It's a wonderful printing job." He shook his head in disbelief. "Please thank your staff for me."

Jackson watched the old man as he lovingly lifted out more and more identical brochures. Smiling, Jackson bowed deeply to Arthur. "It's an honor to serve Rosemary's grandfather."

Rosemary watched Jackson's bow, fascinated. "Is that what you do to your grandfather? Bow like that?"

"No," Jackson confessed. "I saw that on TV. I want your grandfather to know I honor him."

"Thank you, Jackson," Arthur replied softly. "And I honor you, too."

"Well, Grandpa, we have to get back to the shop," Rosemary said, "but now you can stare at your brochures until I get home. Have fun!"

The publication of the brochure gave Arthur his final upward push. His leaflet turned out to be one of the most appealing publications the SPCA had ever used, and Arthur and Gretchen suddenly found themselves in great demand.

More and more, Arthur found himself saying to Rosemary, "I may not be here until four today because Gretchen and I are guests at the hospitality hour at Bayview," or "the recreation time at Sheltering Pines," or "the sing-along at Ridgemont." He always came home from these events enthusiastic and eager to share things the patients had said.

Meantime, Rosemary's end of the scale sank so low that she almost tumbled off. In contrast to Arthur's newly purposeful days, Rosemary's own began to seem newly pointless. Aside from her evenings working with her friends at the print and copy center, the rest of Rosemary's week was spent "putting in time" at school.

For the first time since the loss of Della, she was forced to confront the vacuum in her life that had come with the loss of the loving woman who had been both mother and grandmother to her for nearly seventeen years. No longer could her own empty feelings be shelved on the grounds that her grandfather's crises were more dramatic, or pressing, or life-threatening.

Rosemary dragged around listlessly, not bothering to go running, not seeking out Kevin, slipping deeper and deeper into some remote inner world.

Kevin made friendly overtures, but Rosemary's growing indifference eventually forced him to leave her alone for a while to somehow find her own way out.

At last, on a Monday in mid-December, having decided it was necessary to initiate a new rescue strategy, Kevin waited in the courtyard until Rosemary came out of school, and fell into step beside her.

"How have you been?" he asked.

"Fair," she replied lifelessly.

"How's your grandfather getting along at the nursing homes?"

"Fine." Rosemary dismissed that opener with another one-word response.

Kevin took a deep breath and plunged into what he sensed would be icy waters.

"Have you heard about the party Tanya Selu is giving next Saturday at her uncle's beach house, for any juniors and seniors who want to come?"

"Yeah, I heard." Rosemary's tone was flat. Her answer was designed to close the subject.

The waters were icier than Kevin had expected. Rosemary was remote and inaccessible.

"I'd like to take you to it, Rosemary."

"I don't want to go to a party."

"Why not? It could be fun."

"It'll just be a lot of drinking, and I don't call that fun."

"You don't have to drink. There are a lot of other things to do at a party, you know. I thought we could have a good time if we both went."

"I don't want to go to a party, Kevin!"

Kevin had one move left, and although he had been reluctant to use it, he now hoped its shock value might be beneficial.

"Okay," he said, turning to walk away, "then you won't mind if I take Lisa."

Without waiting for a response from Rosemary, Kevin was gone.

Rosemary was stunned. For a moment she stood there, gathering her senses. Slowly she began to come alive. The words resounded in her mind. Then you won't mind if I take Lisa . . . mind if I take Lisa . . . take Lisa . . . who's Lisa? What became of Yvette? Rosemary's challenge for the next day was to find out who Lisa was.

The minute she met Shirley at lunchtime on Tuesday, she started her sleuthing.

"Shirley, do you know someone, probably new to the school, named Lisa?"

"I don't know her, but I know who she is."

"You do?"

"Everyone knows who she is, Rosemary."

"Everyone? How come I don't?"

"You have not been looking lately."

"What does this Lisa look like?"

Shirley rolled her eyes. "Yellow hair, beautiful eyes, wonderful figure, designer clothes. Her father's a big European businessman. You haven't seen her, Rosemary?" Shirley shook her head in disbelief. "Lisa is the kind of girl who makes the rest of us feel like . . ." Shirley whipped out her dictionary. "Like clumsy."

"Like clumsy." Rosemary's shoulders sagged. "Great. Like clumsy."

Rosemary and Shirley were just starting through the cafeteria line when Shirley suddenly spotted Lisa.

"There she is," she whispered. "She is just now sitting down, next to Kevin."

Rosemary's chin dropped. Lisa didn't need a Newcomers Service Club to make her feel at home. She looked as if she would be in charge of any situation in any one of five languages. She had the poise of a jet-setter and the looks of a model.

"Whew! That's Lisa, huh?" Rosemary felt outclassed, outshone, and outdone. Her pride was wounded. Jealousy was consuming her. That's who he's taking to the party? There has to be a way to get even, she thought irrationally.

In a rash stroke of poor judgment, Rosemary passed by a table near Kevin's, where Frank Mulroy was sitting alone.

Frank had made friendly overtures to Rosemary a number of times after their initial encounter in the ice cream shop, never quite perceiving that she wasn't his type at all.

"Hello, Frank," Rosemary said in a way that she hoped would sound interesting to Frank. "You're looking good. How have you been?"

Frank, surprised by the sudden attention, rose to the occasion.

"Fine, Rosemary. You're looking great yourself."

"Well, see you in seventh period," Rosemary said with a little wave. Out of the corner of her eye she was keeping track of Kevin, wanting him to notice. As she walked past Kevin and Lisa, she started an animated conversation with Shirley, which carried them to the cafeteria door. There Shirley stopped Rosemary's chatter to ask bluntly, "Do you like that Frank?"

"Not really."

"Were you trying to make Kevin angry?"

"Something like that."

Shirley gave Rosemary an understanding smile as they parted.

Rosemary began to wonder exactly what she would do in seventh period, now that she had put the machinery in motion. When the time arrived, however, Frank took over, and Rosemary could only respond. He walked in the door with a purposeful stride and detoured past Rosemary's desk. He got right to the point.

"Wanna go with me to the party at Tanya Selu's next Saturday night? I got a new paint job on my car."

"Yeah, why not," Rosemary agreed.

"So where do you live?"

Rosemary wrote down her address and phone number and handed the paper to Frank.

"What time, Frank?"

"Around six."

Feeling numb, Rosemary nodded. That'll show Kevin, she thought with perverse satisfaction.

For the rest of the week Rosemary tried to ignore her sense of impending disaster. She tried not to think about Saturday. She said almost nothing to Arthur about the forthcoming party, except that it was a junior-senior activity, and that Frank Mulroy was going to give her a ride.

"Why isn't Kevin driving?" Arthur wanted to know.

"He has other plans."

"Are you certain this Frank is safe?"

"Oh sure, Grandpa. He loves his car. He wouldn't do anything to wreck it. Don't worry." Rosemary brushed off the whole event as unimportant. "It's no big thing—it's not a couples' party."

Although Rosemary tried to sound casual, she didn't actually feel that way. The dramatic consequences of her impulsive little scheme were looming ahead. Saturday was payoff day.

Rosemary went out of her way to avoid Kevin until Friday, and then she dropped her carefully crafted one-liner.

"I guess Frank and I will see you and Lisa at the party, Kevin."

Kevin looked stunned. "Frank who?"

"Frank Mulroy, of course. You're taking Lisa. Frank is taking me."

"Frank Mulroy! Why would you go anywhere with Frank Mulroy when you know his reputation? Why would he even ask a girl who doesn't drink?"

Rosemary shrugged and walked away, thoroughly miserable. I didn't know he had a reputation, she stewed. What is his reputation? Her desire to spite Kevin was becoming tinged with fear. Go to a beach house with Frank Mulroy? Drive down Coast Highway 7 with Frank Mulroy? I don't know Frank Mulroy! Rosemary clapped her hand over her mouth.

Then her jealousy flared up again. But, if Kevin's with that Lisa, I don't plan to sit around and be ignored. At least he's noticing! Rosemary had a sense of achievement. Yes, he's certainly noticing.

On Saturday, Rosemary moved mechanically through the day, completing her share of the household duties, finishing her homework, and playing in the yard with Gretchen. At five o'clock she showered, put on the dress that Della had given her on her sixteenth birthday, and waited with a sinking feeling for Frank to appear.

Though crumbling rapidly inside, Rosemary kept reassuring a very nervous Arthur.

"It's okay, Grandpa, I'll be fine. I'm a big girl. Yes, I'll call you if I should need a ride home for any reason."

Rosemary melted with that offer from her grandfather. She gave Arthur a hug. "Thanks, Grandpa. It's nice to have one man I can always count on."

At six o'clock a flashy late-model car with Frank Mulroy at the wheel came careening onto Muirwood Way, making a

U-turn and screeching to a stop outside the Magnuson house. Frank sat there, leaning on his horn, his car stereo blaring, his motor racing.

Rosemary watched the scene with disbelief, goose bumps rising on her skin. I'm going out with this guy?

Arthur was going to pieces. "You can't go off with someone who drives like that, Rosemary."

"Oh, he's just showing off, Grandpa. He'll calm down when we get off the block." Rosemary wished she believed it.

Since Rosemary hadn't responded to his honking, Frank reluctantly got out of the car and ambled to the door. His walk was loose and lazy, as if it was all too much trouble.

Rosemary introduced Frank to Arthur and hastily ushered him out the door before her grandfather could decide how best to intervene.

"Bye, Grandpa," she called to him as she got in the car. The distress on Arthur's face was hard to erase from her mind, but Frank's takeoff shoved all else into the background. His car roared off with a squeal, leaving a trail of rubber on the street. The sound sent shivers down Rosemary's spine. And that's his good driving, she thought with sudden terror. He hasn't even started his serious drinking yet.

Frank switched radio stations, looking for the loudest, and turned it to earsplitting volume. Well, Rosemary thought, we certainly don't have to worry about conversation.

She closed her eyes as the car sped down the winding highway toward the ocean. Frank careened to a stop at the bottom of the grade, where the road suddenly made a sharp turn southward. Rosemary was sure she was going to be sick.

"Where do we go?" Frank shouted over the radio, without slowing down.

"Tanya's place is across the highway from the bait shop on the beach." Rosemary's voice was almost too weak to be heard. "It's coming up soon." She motioned to get her message through.

Frank made the turn into the parking area in front of Tanya's uncle's house without slowing down. He screeched to a stop, his stereo still blaring, and nudged Rosemary with his elbow. "Open your eyes—we're here. Good ride, huh?"

When Rosemary opened her eyes, Kevin and Lisa were standing nearby, staring at the spectacle. She began to tremble. I wanted Kevin to notice us, she thought. How could he possibly not notice us? We're here, Kevin and Lisa, time to notice Rosemary and Frank.

Rosemary opened the car door to step out, but quickly grabbed the car for support. Her rubbery knees wouldn't hold her up. See, I'm here, Kevin and Lisa, she thought grimly.

❧ Chapter 24 ❧

While Kevin watched from a distance as Rosemary regained her walking legs, Lisa descended on Frank's showy car like a well-groomed vulture.

"How gorgeous!" she cooed. Her red-tipped fingers caressed the car's slick finish, which gleamed under the floodlights of the parking area. "Does it go fast?"

"Does it go fast!" Frank's response was instinctive and primitive. "Nobody beats Frank Mulroy!" Then, realizing it had come out like a sullen boast, he polished up his opening for Lisa.

"Pardon me, I should introduce myself. I'm Frank Mulroy."

"I gathered that. I'm Lisa Steuben." She gave Frank an appraising look and tossed her blonde hair back from her face. "You have a fine finish on your fast car, Frank."

"Yeah. You like customizing?"

Lisa had opened the door to admire the upholstery with the dome light on. "Oh, the interior is customized, too."

"Like it?" Frank was bursting with pride. "Come on, I'll take you for a little ride."

Lisa sprang into action. "Wonderful! I'll just be a moment." She walked over to Kevin and flashed a dazzling smile. "You don't mind if I take a little ride in Frank's car, do you, darling? You go on in and have a wonderful time." With a carefully calculated wave, she climbed into Frank's car and began switching radio stations.

Frank turned to Rosemary. "I'm going to let Lisa tell me how my car compares with the European cars. Go ahead and join the party."

Frank climbed in beside Lisa, gunned his motor, and hurtled out of the driveway.

Rosemary, standing alone in the middle of the parking area, watched the taillights rapidly vanish. The few witnesses to the scene had disappeared in embarrassment.

Kevin sauntered over to Rosemary, and, with a toss of his head, motioned for her to come with him.

"Let's go look at the ocean," he said softly.

They crossed the highway and walked beyond the bait shop to the water's edge. Leaning their elbows on the seawall, they silently stared down at the waves as they crashed below in the darkness.

"What were you trying to prove?" Kevin asked after a long silence.

"I wish I could remember," Rosemary replied, her voice barely audible.

"Didn't you know what Frank was like?"

"No, I really didn't."

Kevin shook his head in dismay and gazed out at the dark sea. After a while he asked, "How was your ride down here?"

"You saw our arrival."

From that clue, Kevin could imagine the rest.

"It takes a Lisa to fully appreciate Frank's driving," he said. Half smiling at some image that had just crossed his mind, he chuckled and seemed lost in thought.

"You should have seen the look on her face when I showed up at her place in my mother's little no-nonsense car without a radio. I'm sure she wanted to hide so no one would see her in it."

Kevin was amused. "You see, Rosemary, the difference between you and me is that I knew I'd be dumped the minute something flashy showed up. But you—you seemed surprised when Frank did it to you."

Rosemary smiled wanly without responding.

"Do you still want to go to Tanya's party?" he asked.

"I never wanted to go to her party in the first place."

"Yeah, I do recall that." Kevin continued to look down at the waves. Their eyes hadn't met. "Why don't I go and tell Tanya that we won't be at the party, and then we can take off. Want to?"

"Okay."

"If, by any chance, Frank and Lisa ever show up, Tanya can

give them our regrets." Kevin was going to cover the possibilities.

"They won't show up." Rosemary was realistic. "They're probably in the Sunset Lounge now, having one-for-the-road."

"Yeah, we can forget about them."

Together they stared into the darkness. Kevin put a hand on Rosemary's arm. "You can wait here if you want. I'll swing around with the car in just a moment." He strode off toward the lights and music of Tanya's party.

By herself in the shadows, with the waves breaking below her and an offshore bell buoy tolling its plaintive warning, Rosemary took a deep breath and shivered. The ocean at night was so beautiful and so hard to understand.

Just like my feelings for Kevin, she thought. There's so much that's beyond my control.

What if I should start to love him and then lose him? A chill passed over Rosemary. Her recent encounters with loss and near-loss had left their marks.

I could really fall in love with Kevin now. I know I could. But do I want to take a chance?

He's been falling in love with me for years. I know he has. But should I let him go on to the next level? I don't ever want to hurt Kevin. And I don't want to hurt myself, either. Do I really want to run the risk of loving him?

Sensing that the evening ahead was going to bring both of them to some kind of turning point, Rosemary frantically tried to sort things out while she was alone.

Kevin's car swung into the bait shop parking lot, its headlights sweeping the weather-beaten old structure. Rosemary climbed in beside him and leaned her head against the head-rest, feeling drained.

"Since we're not getting dinner at the party, I'd love to take you to the Whaler's Inn," Kevin said, glancing over at Rosemary. "But I don't have enough money with me. I'd already paid for dinner at Tanya's, so I figured I wouldn't need much."

"Well, why don't I add my money to yours and see what we can afford." Rosemary liked the kind of honesty she and Kevin had always shared. "I brought money because I figured I might need to take care of myself, going out with Frank."

"At least you got that much right about him," Kevin commented.

They spread out their bills and began to plan.

"We could go to the Whaler's Inn and choose very carefully," Kevin said, "or we could go to the Chowder House and eat a lot. Which would you rather do?"

"Let's make it the Whaler's Inn," Rosemary said. "A crab salad and candlelight will be enough for me. What about you?"

"I could be happy with French bread and Rosemary Magnuson's company."

"That's nice, Kev. Thanks."

Kevin pulled onto the coast highway and headed south. The road stayed near the ocean, sometimes running close to a sandy beach and sometimes rising high above the water, clinging to the edge of the cliffs. The beach communities were several miles apart, connected by long stretches of dark roads. Kevin's headlights cut through the darkness, only occasionally meeting an oncoming pair of lights.

On one of the dark stretches, Kevin looked over at Rosemary, all scrunched up in the seat. "You cold? I'll turn on the heat."

Rosemary was shivering, but not from the cold. She could feel things happening between them. Tonight the chemistry was different. She knew it.

When the lights of the Whaler's Inn shone ahead, Rosemary wondered if she would even feel like eating a crab salad. Her stomach was a tight knot. Kevin gave her a reassuring smile and turned in at the inn's crowded parking lot. He eased into the only space left, right next to the seawall, and turned off his engine. A large wave broke below them, sending spray over Rosemary's side of the car.

"Maybe you'd better get out on my side," he suggested. "It's a little more sheltered."

Kevin got out first and held the door, while Rosemary scooted over. Her dress clung to the upholstery, pulling it well above her knees. Feeling suddenly shy, she tugged at her skirt. Then she caught the humor in her gesture. Kevin has seen me in swimming suits since I was six years old, she thought. What am I hiding from him tonight?

Kevin smiled and offered Rosemary his hand as she stepped from the car. They walked hand-in-hand to the entrance of the Whaler's Inn and opened the weathered mahogany door.

While the hostess was putting Kevin's name on the waiting list, Rosemary went to the ladies' room. After staring for a moment at her image in the full-length mirror, she decided that Kevin and the Whaler's Inn deserved more. Not having put much enthusiasm into her earlier grooming to go out with Frank Mulroy, Rosemary now plunged into a serious overhaul. She lined up her materials at the makeup table and went to work. The transformation was pleasing, even to Rosemary. With a new glow, she stepped out to meet Kevin. He took one look and drew in his breath with obvious approval.

"Let's go over and sit down by the windows," he said. "We have about a twenty-minute wait." He led the way to the large picture window at the far end of the cocktail lounge. As they sat on a little loveseat facing the water, Rosemary was enchanted with the reflections on the windows. She could see the tables in the dining room behind them, each with a bouquet of fresh flowers. Old-fashioned lamps cast dancing shadows on the faces of the diners.

"I love it," she whispered to Kevin. "I'll eat less than a crab salad, if necessary."

"No, we're okay. I checked the menu. We can even have dinner, if we read the entrees from the bottom up."

Rosemary felt like royalty when a hostess led the way to a table, seated her across from Kevin, and said a waiter would come soon for their orders. She glanced over the top of the menu, over the fresh flowers, over the glow lamp, and studied the young man across the table. Is this the same Kevin Melero? Those soft eyes, that half smile around the mouth, that well-styled wavy hair with a front lock that refuses to conform. This is not the boy I grew up with. Rosemary smiled, unable to hide her approval.

"You look nice, Kevin."

"Thanks. I was thinking the same about you."

They didn't talk very much during dinner, but it was a comfortable silence. Now and then their eyes met, exchanging messages of approval. Finally, the waiter cleared away their plates and brought a dessert menu.

"Blueberry cheesecake sounds good," Rosemary mused. She caught a look of panic on Kevin's face. "No," she said, "I guess I don't want anything, thanks."

The waiter, sizing up the situation, turned to Kevin. "And you, sir?"

"Let's have one blueberry cheesecake." Kevin's response was carefully calculated.

"And two plates?" the waiter asked.

"That would be fine," Kevin agreed, grinning.

They lingered over their half slices of cheesecake as long as they could, but they finally had to admit that dinner was over. With reluctance, they left the dining room and stepped out into the chill night air of the parking lot.

The tide had risen and the breakers were splashing the cars nearest the seawall.

"We're going to have to make a dash for it between waves," Kevin said. "I'll go first and unlock your door."

Rosemary watched for her chance and scurried to the car, getting the door closed just as a giant breaker sent a plume of spray into the parking lot. Snug inside, they watched the reflected light from the inn sparkling on the droplets that trickled down the windshield.

Kevin put his arm across Rosemary's shoulders and pulled her closer.

"We've changed, Rosie. All during dinner I was wishing I had you in my arms."

"All during dinner I was thinking how nice that would be, Kev."

Kevin leaned over and kissed Rosemary, tentatively at first, waiting for a response. When it was clear that Rosemary shared his feelings, they kissed long and tenderly.

Finally, Rosemary pulled away, surprised at how hard it was to stop.

"We *have* changed," she said softly. "Somewhere along the way, the kids from Muirwood Way grew up."

"I've been in love with you for years, Rosemary," Kevin confessed. "I've been waiting a long time." He looked squarely at her. "Have I gotten lucky enough at last to have you falling in love with me?"

"I think I am, Kev. In fact, I know I am, and it scares me to death."

"Why? Love isn't that dangerous."

"Yes it is! To me, at least. I've just lost someone I loved, and I came close to losing a second one, and I don't even want to think about loving and losing again."

Kevin put both arms around Rosemary and held her close, stroking her hair softly.

"Life doesn't come with any guarantees, Rosie. There will always be some risks, and if you aren't willing to run some risks, the alternative is to feel nothing. But that means no joy, either. That's the price. Do you really want to be that safe?"

"No."

"Then welcome to the world of the walking wounded. There are worse things than wounds—wounds heal."

Rosemary wiped away a tear that was rolling down her cheek.

"Come on, run the risk, Rosie. Let yourself love. Love me like I love you."

"Give me time, Kev. I'm getting there."

Kevin kissed Rosemary again, very gently. Soon he turned on the ignition and started the car.

As they left the Whaler's Inn behind and headed north again, Rosemary and Kevin both looked back for one last glimpse of the place that had become special to them. They drove in quiet.

The long dark stretches of road gave them time for uninterrupted thinking. By the time they reached Muirwood Way, the newness of their feelings had begun to have some reality.

Kevin stopped in front of Rosemary's house and leaned over for a last kiss of the evening.

"Want to come in?" she asked him.

"No, I think your grandpa needs you to himself now. I'll see you tomorrow."

"All right."

"You going to tell him anything about us tonight?"

"Mmmn. Maybe. If I can think of a way to break it to him gently."

"Yeah, there's always a problem when a woman falls in love with someone who doesn't have family approval."

Rosemary chuckled at Kevin's absolute certainty of his standing with Arthur

"But you know that Grandpa's always felt I should fall in love with that kid down the street."

"And .. ?"

"And instead, I fell in love with the man down the street." Kevin grinned.

"Good-night, Rosie. *My* Rosie."

"Kevin, I've told you a million . . ." Rosemary's voice trailed off into a sigh. "The name's Rosie."

♫ Chapter 25 ♫

Rosemary took Arthur by surprise when she opened the front door. He and Gretchen were watching a TV movie and looked very comfortable in the armchair.

"Rosemary! I didn't hear you. I was sure I would know when Frank's car drove up. If I missed the engine noise, the stereo would certainly announce his arrival."

"That's true, Grandpa, it would." Rosemary could smile about the situation now. "But Frank's car is somewhere speeding along the coast with Frank and Lisa in it, instead of Frank and Rosemary."

Arthur was nervously studying Rosemary's face for signs of heartbreak.

"Are you all right? Who brought you home?"

"Kevin."

"Your escort went off with another girl?"

"I think the word is 'dumped,' Grandpa. Yes, Frank dumped me."

"My goodness." Arthur's features changed as he was suddenly reminded of some long-forgotten incident. "I remember Della got into a funny situation once, at the church social." He was smiling as he retrieved an old memory.

Rosemary was intrigued. "Gram? I didn't think things were the same in those days."

"Some things never change, Rosemary. There have always been dumpers. Come into the kitchen and I'll tell you about it over some hot chocolate." Arthur removed Gretchen from his lap and got up stiffly.

"This was a Fourth of July party at the church," he began, fixing the cocoa as he talked. "Della was eighteen and I was twenty. Oh, she was a bright, spunky girl. I had been admiring her for a long time, and I was hoping I could take her to the party. But I was too shy, and Wilton Greathouse asked her first."

"You blew it, huh?" Rosemary was eager to hear more.

Arthur brought the hot mugs to the table and went on. "I went to the party alone, nursing my wounds. Well, a new girl in town showed up at the party—Isabelle Roget. She was gorgeous, no doubt about it, and Wilton spotted her as she came in the door. Within an hour, Wilton and Isabelle had disappeared, and Della knew she had been jilted."

"Oh-oh, what did she do?"

"She was seething, of course, but I stepped in and asked her if she'd let me take her home. She agreed, eager to get away from the scene of her humiliation."

"So you took her home?"

"Rosemary! Give me credit for a little more life than that. We drove to a lookout point above the city, and . . . and counted stars."

"And?"

"And we became best friends, and eventually got married."

"And lived happily ever after."

"No, we had to earn our happiness, Rosemary. Really, truly earn it. I had some things to learn, and so did she. Della was a high-spirited, independent lady, you know, long before women's lib came onto the scene. She needed room to grow and function in her own right, or there would have been no happiness in our marriage."

Arthur's gaze was fastened on some distant point beyond Rosemary. "Actually," he mused, "there were three parties in our marriage: Della, Arthur, and the team of Della and Arthur. Together we formed a third person, stronger than either of us could ever have been alone." Arthur glanced at Rosemary to see if what he had just said made sense. "We had to be strong, you know, to get through the loss of your beautiful mother." His eyes grew misty.

"Somehow, it didn't seem that hard for you to be happy with Gram," Rosemary responded. "You hardly ever fought, at least not in front of me."

"Well, since we loved each other, we each tried to do what would be right for the other person," Arthur explained. "That way it was usually a conflict of love and concern."

Rosemary stared into her empty cocoa mug, lost in a new idea. Arthur, cherishing his memories, retreated into silence.

When Rosemary finally spoke, it was with a fresh respect for the man who had brought her up so lovingly.

"Grandpa, I've got to learn what you know about caring for someone."

Arthur, his eyes brimming with tears, looked tenderly at his granddaughter and nodded.

"You start by being friends, Rosemary. That's where it all begins. Best friends, then lovers."

"Then I really am home free, Grandpa. I'm home free, at last."

Arthur raised a questioning eyebrow. "Oh?"

Rosemary ducked her head.

"And have you picked out the person you're going to care for?" Arthur asked gently.

"Maybe."

"Would it be Kevin, by any chance?"

Rosemary nodded solemnly. Breaking into a smile, she said, "I know, Grandpa, I know. You told me long ago—he's true blue, through and through. But some things I have to learn the stupid way. You know me."

"Yes, Rosemary, I know you," Arthur replied, his voice choking slightly. "And for almost seventeen years I've thanked God for that privilege."

Rosemary and her grandfather exchanged shy glances across the table. Feeling awkward, Arthur picked up the mugs and took them to the sink. Rosemary reached for a towel to wipe the table.

"Are you and Gretchen going to finish your movie?" she asked, bringing the conversation back to a safer subject.

"No, now that you're in, I think I'll go to bed."

"Me, too."

They turned out the lights and walked together down the hall. When Rosemary turned on the light in her room, she gasped.

"Grandpa! What have you been up to?" She could hardly grasp the scene. The antique Swedish music box had been refinished and was sitting on her desk. Benjamin Bear was standing by the music box, his paw poised to operate it. And every other bear in Rosemary's collection was perched in some unexpected place nearby, watching.

"Grandpa!" Rosemary rushed to give her beaming grandfather a hug. "You refinished the music box for me?"

"It's yours now, Rosemary, a reminder of your Swedish heritage, you know."

"I love it! I love you, Grandpa!"

Rosemary glanced back at the bear scene.

"And the bears . . ." She wiped away a tear. "I thought nobody would ever play bear games with me again. I didn't know you liked bears, Grandpa."

"I like granddaughters," Arthur replied. He retreated, wiping his eyes.

Rosemary went over and studied each inspired bear pose. Instinctively, she started to pick up Benjamin, then drew back. He and all his bear friends would stay exactly as Arthur had placed them, a touching reminder that she was still someone's cherished granddaughter.

For a while Rosemary sat dreamily on her bed, imagining a dignified silver-haired gentleman delicately bending Muffin's legs to make him sit on the stamp box, hooking Andrew's stuffed paw through the shade pull, perching Alicia's chubby body on the Paddington Bear books. She grinned. Gram's influence, still with him, always a part of him. I wonder . . . thirty-five years from now. Rosemary's mind was drifting back to the look in Kevin's eyes as he sat across from her at the Whaler's Inn.

Unaware of her motions, she mechanically hung her dress in the closet and prepared for bed. After turning off the light and crawling between the smooth sheets, she lifted her head for one last look at Benjamin, standing on the desk in the moonlight, playing with his music box.

For a moment Rosemary lay in the dark, alone with her thoughts. Then, needing reassurance that her grandfather was near, she quietly tiptoed across the room and opened the door to the darkened hallway.

Arthur's light was out, but Gretchen was still stirring. Rosemary could hear her grandfather whispering to the dog, as he so often did lately. It had become his way of thinking out loud.

"Gretchen, come and settle down."

There was a scurrying of feet and a soft plop as the little dog landed on the bed. "Now shush, little girl," Arthur murmured. "I have memories to sort out in my mind. Tonight I've been reminded of priceless moments."

For a time there was silence in his room, but soon a muffled narration began, punctuated by long silences. From her own treasure trove of family lore, Rosemary picked out the moments she was sure her grandfather would be cherishing. She had grown up loving his stories. Of course there would be the young Arthur, eager to take Della to the social and losing out on the first round.

There would be the perky, independent Della, discovering the charms of the immigrant lad with limited English.

And there would be Della, moving through the years, the radiant bride, the serene new mother, the mother-of-the-bride, the proud grandmother.

There would be grief—Della and Arthur weeping at the graves of Susan and Charles, promising to rear their only child.

And then there would be Rosemary, at three with bears, at nine with roller skates, at thirteen with a paper route, at sixteen placing two red roses on Della's casket.

Arthur's voice, across the hall, became louder and his words more distinct, enabling Rosemary to catch bits of the conversation. No longer was he mumbling to Gretchen—he was addressing his wife.

"Life is so uncertain, isn't it, Della? But which of these moments would I give up just because they wouldn't last forever?"

In the darkness Rosemary heard her grandfather chuckling. "Did you see it, Della? Did you see what I did with Rosemary's bears? I'm not doing badly, Della. You'd be proud of me."

Feeling that perhaps she had intruded too much, Rosemary tiptoed to her door and closed it quietly, patting Benjamin's furry head and rearranging Alicia's skirt as she passed the desk.

She slipped back into bed with memories of her own to sort out. Some of the images were blurry, going back ten years, seven years, five—kindergarten and Kevin protecting her, third grade and Kevin teasing her, sixth grade and Kevin challenging her, ninth grade and doing homework together.

Rosemary curled up in a ball, hugging her pillow as her mind drifted on.

The look on Kevin's face when Frank left me standing there in the parking lot. The way he managed it so I wouldn't have to face the other kids. His noticing that I was shivering on the way to the Whaler's Inn. Did he know why I was shivering? His keeping a straight face when I was pulling down my skirt.

As the most special images came into focus, Rosemary clung to each one, examining it minutely, savoring every delicate detail.

Kevin with candlelight shadows dancing on his face . . . Kevin ordering one slice of blueberry cheesecake and two plates . . . Kevin's arms around her . . . Kevin's kiss . . . Kevin . . . Kevin . . . Most of all, Kevin trying to discipline that front lock of hair.

Rosemary saw it so clearly. Kevin at every age—six, nine, twelve, eighteen, tossing his head to control his dark, silky hair.

"Quit trying," Rosemary murmured drowsily. "I like it that way. Leave it free, Kev. It's nice . . . it's . . . nice . . ."

Phyllis Anderson Wood writes with a special understanding of teenagers that stems from twenty-five years of close listening in the classroom. She teaches English and reading at Westmoor High School in Daly City, California, near San Francisco.

The daughter of a high school principal, Mrs. Wood grew up in San Francisco and did her undergraduate work at the University of California at Berkeley and graduate work at Stanford University. She and her husband of thirty-eight years live in South San Francisco, and enjoy having their daughter and two sons living in the Bay Area.

Phyllis Anderson Wood is the author of eleven novels, among them *A Five-color Buick and a Blue-eyed Cat, Win Me and You Lose*, and *Pass Me a Pine Cone*. Her understanding of family relationships and teenage anxieties have made them popular young adult reading.